Getting Lucky in London

by

Darah Lace

This is a work of fiction. Names, characters, places, and incidents are either the product of the author's imagination or are used fictitiously, and any resemblance to actual persons living or dead, business establishments, events, or locales, is entirely coincidental.

Getting Lucky in London ~ Copyright 2022 by Darah Lace

Cover Art by *Diana Carlile*

http://www.designingdiana.blogspot.com

Published in the United States of America

Dedication

To anyone who has ever found romance on foreign ground...literally or figuratively.

Chapter One

Danielle

ROLLING MY SUITCASE behind me, I stepped inside my brother's flat in Chelsea, just outside central London, and then right into his outspread arms. Three years had passed since Dominic left New York after I graduated from college, and though we talked once a week, it wasn't the same. "I've missed you."

"Missed you, too, Daisy." His use of my nickname was as warm and comforting as his embrace, and it soothed my guilt for intruding at such short notice. Only he had ever called me Daisy, never Danielle like our mother did or Dani like my friends and coworkers.

He kissed the top of my head and stepped back. "You look great."

"You're sweet, but look at *you*."

His tall, lanky frame had filled out, more man now than the boy he'd been before moving. He looked like the pictures of our dad when he was young—jet black hair, deep brown eyes, and chiseled features that rivaled the angels. But telling him that would put a damper on their reunion, and the nervous energy rolling off him was bad enough.

"I'm sorry, Daize. I feel really bad about not picking you up at the airport. And for leaving on your first day here."

"You couldn't have predicted Sarah's father would have a heart attack this morning." I folded my arms across my ribs and gave him a you've-been-keeping-secrets-from-me look. "I didn't realize things were that serious between you two."

"Neither did I." A lopsided grin split his face. "But I can't let her go alone." He grabbed my hand. "Come on."

He led me past the living room and into the small kitchen at the back of the house. He'd only been dating Sarah a few months, so if he was willing to miss work for her, he had to be head over heels. He never missed work. "So is she *the one*?"

"I think so."

I draped the sweater I'd worn on the flight over one of the backless barstools at the counter. "I hope so. You deserve to be happy."

His head tilted to one side. "Are you?"

"Well, if I get the job," I said, placing my purse on top of the sweater, "I'll be happy to be closer to you. It's too long between visits."

He grimaced. "I know, but I promise I'll have my fingers *and* my toes crossed tomorrow, whether I'm still in Cape Town or back here."

"I'm really sorry for coming at such an inconvenient time." The job interview had come out of the blue on Tuesday, and they'd demanded an in-person visit by Friday.

"Stop apologizing." He waved a hand, dismissing my guilt. "I'm just happy to see you."

I hadn't even considered changing jobs, but when this one opened up, I jumped at the chance to live closer to Dominic. All we had was each other. Well, except now, he had Sarah.

The last few days had been a whirlwind. I'd managed to take off work, secure the seven-hour midnight flight out of New York last night so I'd have time to catch my breath before the interview tomorrow, and now, it was—

I looked at my watch. Two p.m. London time. "What time is your flight?"

"Five."

"You'd better get a move on. You don't want to keep Sarah waiting."

As if I'd lit a match under his ass, he disappeared up the stairs, giving me time to look around his new Chelsea digs. This flat was bigger than the tiny place he'd lived in the last time I visited. Definitely nicer. The bottom floor had been remodeled into a popular open-concept design. He'd worked hard to move up the corporate ladder and far beyond the little rundown shack we'd grown up in.

A minute later, Dominic came down the stairs, his luggage *clank, clank, clanking* on each step.

"Your room is the first door off the landing."
He left his suitcase and joined her in the
kitchen. "There's food in the fridge. I stocked it
when you said you were coming. I might not be
here when you leave, so"—he pulled his keys
from his pocket—"take my car if you want to go
anywhere you can't get to by foot or by taxi.
Sightseeing in the country or whatever."

I'd seen the flashy trophy car parked out
front. "Ha! These people drive on the wrong side
of the road. I'm not risking your new baby."

"Oh thank God."

I chuckled at the relief on his face. I was a
terrible driver and had the record to prove it, so
his feelings were totally justified. Besides,
sightseeing alone was boring, but I wouldn't tell
him that. He'd just feel guiltier than he already
did for leaving. Another thing we had in
common—guilt for everything and anything.

Dominic tapped an envelope on the counter.
"Sarah and I wanted to take you out tonight. I
bought four tickets to an art exhibit at a local
gallery. We thought you'd like it. I gave one to
Michael, but there are three left if you want to
ask someone from the museum."

My heart thudded to a stop and then
thundered into a gallop. I swallowed. "Who?"

"Michael Winters. You remember him,
right? We played football together."

Remember him? Like I could ever forget.
He'd been the love of my life as a teen, though
only from afar. I'd met him once but hadn't seen

him in eleven years. And he was here in London. "How did you two reconnect? I mean, you haven't talked about him in years."

"He was the architect on the remodel for this place when I bought it, and we've been hanging out, getting to know each other again." His gaze scanned the two rooms. "I thought I told you."

"No." I definitely would have remembered.

He shrugged. "Anyway, I told him you'd be there with us, but I'll let him know you'll be alone. I'm sure he'll be happy to show you around."

The last thing I wanted was Michael Winters obligated to hang out with me, to babysit Dominic's little sister.

"You should go to the show," Dominic went on. "Get out. Have fun."

Panic bubbled inside me, but I tamped it down. I'd never told my brother about the silly crush I'd had on Michael. Dominic needed a friend back then, and I couldn't jeopardize that with a teenage infatuation.

I faked a yawn. "I'll probably just crash. It's been a long day...er, night."

"Well, if you change your mind, there's money in here, too, for a cab." He gave the envelope another tap.

"What am I? Twelve?"

He picked up his keys and put them in his pocket, then shook his head and pulled them out again. Flipping past the little black fob and a half dozen keys, he picked out the square one. "This opens the deadbolt. Be sure to lock up when you leave and especially while you're here alone."

I started to tell him I was twenty-four fucking years old, a grown-ass woman, and he knew full well I'd taken over the parenting role as soon as he left for college. And I'd moved to New York and been living on my own since our mother died of alcohol poisoning, just before he'd taken off three years ago to finally live his dream.

He held up a hand. "It's a safe neighborhood, but you never know."

He'd been overprotective since our father skipped out on us when I was five and he was ten. I'd picked daisies every day for a year and plucked the petals to see if my daddy would come back.

Every day, Dominic would ask, "Well, Daisy, what do you say today?"

No matter the answer, my father never came home. Dominic had donned the role of man of the house, and I had become Daisy.

"Would you just get out of here?" I gave him a teasing shove.

He snagged the handle of his suitcase and made his way to the door. He was halfway out when he turned around. "Love you, Daisy."

"Love you, too." Following him, I shooed him with both hands. "Call me when you get there."

"Will do." He started to shut the door, then

added, "Lock up behind me."

I leaned against the casing as he jogged the four steps from the tiny porch to the sidewalk. "Tell Sarah I hope her father recovers quickly and that I look forward to meeting her."

"I will. Bye," he said with a wave as he climbed into the waiting taxi and shut the door.

"Bye," I whispered, knowing he didn't hear me but needing to say it anyway. I waited for the taxi to pull away, then closed the front door and exhaled a long sigh.

I could feel the jet lag setting in, but I shook it off and went back to the kitchen to collect my things. Unpack first, then a nap. Odds were Dominic didn't own an iron, and my suit probably looked like Grandma Moses' face.

Dominic's key ring caught my attention. Three inches of pewter, it had large chunky letters carved into it and painted with the Union Jack pattern. Curiosity beckoning, I flipped the key ring toward me to read, *Britain's Bitch.*

I smiled. Someone had a sense of humor, but it certainly wasn't Dominic. Sarah? I hoped so. He needed someone to yank the serious out of him now and then.

My fingers brushed the envelope containing tickets to the exhibit, but it wasn't the art on display that made my insides swirl. Michael Chandler Winters, Three Time All-American Wide Receiver turned highly sought-after architect.

Dominic had received a football scholarship at a university five hundred and fifty-some-odd miles away from our little hometown near Tulsa, Oklahoma, and I'd missed three seasons. I'd only been able to watch him play on TV if the network picked up the game. My mother blew every penny she received from welfare on booze and cigarettes.

His third year in college—my junior year in high school—I took on a part time job, scrimped and saved where I could, and finally earned enough money for a round-trip bus ticket, a hotel for one night, and a ticket to his game. He'd been so excited to have me there, to watch him play in person, but the second he introduced me to his teammate, Michael, I hadn't seen anyone else on the field that day, the rest of that season, or the following.

So silly, the teenage heart. Michael hadn't even noticed me that day, given the fact he had a gorgeous, sorority blonde on his arm.

"Hmph." I tapped the envelope with my index finger. "I hope he's gone bald and fat."

But...what if he *wasn't* fat or bald? What if he was still as delicious as I remembered? And what if I showed him I wasn't the same little girl with stringy hair, crooked teeth, and threadbare clothing? What was the worst thing that could happen?

He could have another gorgeous blonde on his arm.

Or he could be alone. He only had one ticket.

Hmm. Michael Winters all to myself, with no one to keep my naughty in check. That could be dangerous...and a whole lot of yum.

A smile tugged at my lips and excitement scrubbed at the edges of my exhaustion. I couldn't miss the opportunity to finally put my teenage infatuation to bed...literally.

I grabbed my sweater, purse, and suitcase and headed up the stairs for a shower and a little—make that a lot—of primping. I had a fantasy to fulfill.

Michael

THE SUN WAS OUT FOR the first time in days, and the city shone as if it had been washed clean. Yet the bright and cheery view that promised a warm summer afternoon outside my eighth-floor office window did nothing to brighten or cheer my mood as I read my father's text for the third time.

It was short and to the point. Brandon Winters had never held much use for sentimentality, but news like this seemed to warrant at least a phone call. Didn't it?

Dad: *Getting a divorce. Didn't work out with Callie.*

"Bloody hell." Not that I had ever liked Callie. Just as I hadn't liked Jennifer, his third wife. I liked the one in between though— Leeann. She'd been good for my father, made him seem almost human.

The intercom buzzer on my desk turned me from my musings. I spun my chair around to answer, "Yes?"

"Lady Chandler to see you," Jaycee, the receptionist, answered. "Shall I send her in?"

"Please do."

A few seconds later, my mother peeked around the flat panel of mahogany that blended with the walls of my office. Her smile instantly calmed the anger roiling in my gut, which was probably the reason for her visit. She knew everything before I did. Probably heard from one of her friends in the States.

"Do you have time for a chat?" she asked but let herself in anyway and closed the door behind her.

"I always have time for you, Mum." I met her halfway across the room and greeted her with a kiss on the cheek. "What brings you here?"

Her hazel eyes searched my face as she sat in a chair in front of my desk, smoothing slacks that weren't wrinkled. "I wanted to make sure you were all right."

I rounded the desk, lowered myself into my chair, and tried to hide my frustration with a shrug and a smile. I should be used to my father's merry-go-round marriages by now. "I'm fine. I'm only surprised it lasted this long."

My parents' marriage had been turbulent until they came to an agreement that my mother would turn a blind eye to my fathers' extramarital affairs until I graduated high school. Not long after I began my first semester at university, they told me they were getting a divorce and my mother was moving back to England. And as soon as I held my diploma in my hand, I joined her.

I loved my father, but I didn't respect him. And I wanted nothing to do with the family law firm. Instead, I'd made my own way in my mother's country, in her beloved city of London, and in my own preferred career in architecture.

"Well, I know how much it bothers you." She eased forward until she perched on the edge of the chair, concern creasing her otherwise smooth forehead.

I looked away for a moment. I should never have shared my greatest fear with her, that I was too much like my father, that I couldn't have a relationship with a woman longer than it took to learn her name or to hear her moan mine.

That wasn't quite fair. I'd dated a few women longer, possibly a month, maybe six weeks. I'd tried. I really had. But as soon as I

11

knew—usually right away—they weren't the woman I wanted to spend the rest of my life with, I saw no reason to drag out a relationship only to hurt them more.

"You are not like him." She'd never had a bad word to say about my father, but for the first time I could remember, her voice gave a small hint of what I suspected she truly felt—anger, hurt, and disgust.

I sighed and faced the woman I'd seen torn apart every time a new woman took her place in my father's bed. "I'm trying not to be."

In the last year, my attempts to date had been fewer and farther between. At twenty-nine, the yearning for a home and family had grown. I wanted to find a woman I could grow old with. I knew, or at least hoped, she was out there somewhere, but the search was disheartening.

That didn't mean I was dead. I still had needs, and I'd recently ended one of those temporary distractions. It hadn't gone well.

"You haven't been over in a while. Why don't you drop in tonight?" she asked with renewed determination to cheer me up. "I'll cook your favorites, and you and Robbie can talk about the design of your new project."

Robert Townes had hired Michael upon my arrival in London and made me a partner in his firm four years ago. Robert had become the father Brandon Winters could never be. When I introduced Robert to my mother, the attraction between them was palpable. They now lived together, and I'd watched my mother come alive. She was happy, truly happy.

"I'd love to, but I can't." I glanced at my watch. Just enough time to get home and change. "I promised Dominic I'd meet him and Sarah and his little sister at the art exhibit."

"Oh, that sounds lovely." Her eyes brightened, and she rose from her seat. "I won't keep you then."

I stood and followed her to the door.

She rose on tiptoes to kiss my cheek and straightened my tie. "Give Dominic my love and tell him we should all get together soon."

"He'll like that. He's always had a soft spot for you," I teased.

"That's because I spent more time with *him* than with *you* when I came for your games. I suspect he needed a mother figure in his life."

"Yes, and you were great with him." I opened the door for her. "Love you, Mum."

"Love you, darling." She left me feeling much better or, at least, not in the doldrums I'd been in before she arrived.

Returning to my desk, I was suddenly looking forward to going out tonight. I checked my phone for Dominic's reply to my text asking what time to meet him at the gallery. No answer, but it was still early. I'd keep trying. And if Dominic was a no-show, I'd work the room for possible new clients for the firm.

One thing was certain, though. I was bloody well not in the mood for another distraction.

Chapter Two

Danielle

"YER HERE, MISS," the cabbie announced as he braked hard.

Peering out the taxi window at the line of people waiting to get into the gallery, I tried to shake off an onset of nerves threatening to overtake me at the prospect of running into Michael.

"Miss?"

"Sorry." I turned back to the driver. "How much do I owe you?"

He rattled off a figure, and I opened the clutch bag that matched the little black dress I'd packed in case Dominic and Sarah took me out on the town. The purse was only big enough to carry my phone, a tube of red lipstick, my brother's keys, some cash—U.S. dollars, so those were useless to me now, and I'd forgotten the money in the envelope he'd left—and a credit card. I unzipped the compartment where I'd stashed the credit card and pulled out...a condom.

Heat flooded her cheeks. *Jesus, where did that come from?*

The answer came when I read the black writing on the neon yellow wrapper. Mardi Gras two years ago.

"We don't accept those, miss," the driver said and bent forward, cackling, his hand slapping the steering wheel.

Mortified, I shoved the condom back in my purse and pulled out the card. "Here."

Wiping his eyes, he slid it through the reader and handed it back to me. "Sorry, miss. But don't worry. Some young bloke'll be right happy to help ya with that."

I couldn't get out of the cab fast enough. Smoothing my dress, I looked around to make sure no one had witnessed my embarrassment. Everyone seemed absorbed in their own world and totally oblivious to mine. The cab pulled away from the curb, the driver still laughing at my expense.

I hooked the long silver chain of the black clutch over my shoulder and found my place at the end of the line. If the condom fiasco was any indication of the night to come, I should go home now.

Minutes later, I made it through the gallery door, handed my ticket to a sleek brunette in black silk, and mingled with the crowd ranging from young bohemian trendsetters to wealthy, upper class connoisseurs. Carrying flutes of champagne, waiters wove between the gathered cliques.

I grabbed a glass to bolster my waning courage. I'd spent the last few hours talking myself in and out of attending. What difference would seeing Michael make to my life? Then again, I owed it to myself to at least try to have a good time and enjoy his company. But what if he dismissed me again?

In the end, I'd decided to forget Michael, take advantage of the ticket, and check out some of the local artists. If for no other reason than to show my support.

Normally, that would have been enough. Art and all that it entailed fueled my passion, whether oil on a canvas or a sculpture from old car parts. Even graffiti on a train car could hold me spellbound.

Yet now that I was here, art was not what had my pulse racing. Telling myself to forget Michael was easy. Putting that sage advice into practice was altogether different.

I downed the golden bubbly in one gulp, snagged another glass from a passing server's tray, and stopped in front of a structure of silver and blue meant to embody a waterfall. As I rocked from one foot to the other, the strips of metal took on a life of their own, the movement of the water seeming almost real.

Smiling, I glanced up at the painting in the next aisle and froze.

Michael Winters stood ten feet away, chatting with an older couple. To my dismay, he wasn't fat, and he wasn't bald. If possible, he was even more beautiful than he'd been eleven years ago. Tall and lean, but with enough grooves cut in hard muscle to keep a woman's fingers busy for days. Unless they were busy playing with that trademark tawny hair. Every time he'd taken off his helmet on the sideline, I'd itched to get my hands on the unruly waves that weren't quite brown but not blond either.

The man had been a piece of art in a football uniform, but his slim-fitting black slacks outlined long slender legs, trim hips, and a good-sized bulge. A crisp white shirt hugged his chest, shoulders, and arms as if it were made specifically for him. Probably was. He came from money.

Butterflies fluttered in my belly, followed by a cold wash of fear as my gaze journeyed higher to find him...looking right at me.

Shit. Busted. I'd forgotten there was no TV screen to protect me from taking my fill of his hotness. Too far away to read his reaction, I held my breath and waited to see what he'd do.

Nothing. He did nothing.

Should I go over and say hello? No, he was with friends or maybe clients. I couldn't interrupt, and the idea of him feeling obligated to babysit as a favor to Dominic rankled.

I took a sip of champagne, then turned away to casually stroll in the opposite direction.

Ten minutes later, I tried to focus on the showcase piece of the gallery, but all I registered was the big blob of red on a black background. It could have been anything.

I fought the urge to look for Michael. I couldn't stand here all night, but I was afraid to turn around, afraid he'd be there, and I'd behave like the lovestruck fangirl from years ago. Or worse, he'd be gone, my last chance smothered by insecurity.

Slugging back the rest of my champagne to add to the buzz coming on, I swore it would be my last. Two was my limit, and I wanted to keep a clear head. I didn't need any extra help getting to Stupid Town. Just the sight of Michael had me following a big arrow that blinked "*Stupid*" and "*Spineless*" in bright red letters.

Ugh. "Pathetic."

A crackling chuckle came from beside me, and a blue-haired older woman with parchment-thin skin lifted a gnarled finger. "Pathetic, yes, and the color is weak."

So am I.

I shook my head. *Enough already.*

I turned to the woman, hoping for an intelligent conversation—I wasn't having one with myself—but the lady was already shuffling away. I hoped I hadn't just destroyed the artist's chance for a sale.

With a sigh, I forced my feet to move and headed to the stone sculpture to my right. Despite my resolution not to, I slid a glance in Michael's direction. The couple was still there, but he wasn't.

You lost him.

I darted a quick glance to the left of where he'd been, then to the right. *There.*

He'd joined another group of enthusiasts who were oohing and aahing over the waterfall piece, which put him about five feet closer. But he wasn't looking at the metal sculpture. He was looking at me. In particular, at my legs.

Oh, hello. Cream dampened my panties. I'd seen that look in a man's eyes before. He was interested. In me. Well, in my legs, because his gaze hadn't made it back to my face yet. I could work with that. Maybe I'd get that fantasy fulfilled after all.

One of the women, a redhead in her mid-to-late forties, laid a hand on his arm, and his gaze snapped up to meet mine. He smiled that smile I'd seen after every touchdown, and my stomach did a somersault. Giving me a nod and the quirk of a sexy brow, he returned his attention to the woman.

With that look, he'd as much as said he was okay with getting caught returning my perusal and liked what he saw. A rush of heat cascaded through me as reality set in. I wasn't going to have to seduce him. He was doing the seducing. And all he'd had to do was stand there.

Nope. Self-respect demanded that I, at the very least, make him work for it.

Semi-confident he'd do so, I meandered deeper into the gallery, letting myself enjoy and soak in the art.

It only took ten minutes for Michael to show up in the group of people three paintings away. I slipped behind a rather large sculpture with a crack in the design big enough for me to watch him through and not be seen. He carried on a conversation, but his gaze scanned the room, never lighting on any one thing or person too long.

I smiled and my pulse raced. Our game of cat and mouse was as intoxicating as the alcohol.

I stepped toward the next painting that allowed me to face him at an angle. His gaze finally found me, taking me in from head to toe and back again. Someone blocked my view of him though—another woman vying for his attention, this one younger, closer to twenty-five, and blonde...and gorgeous...and flirting with him.

I frowned when the woman looped her arm through his. Was she his girlfriend? She seemed to think so. He sure had a type.

And you're nowhere near it.

I was about to turn away when his gaze cut in my direction and slid over me again, lingering on my breasts. My nipples pebbled, and I bit my lip to keep from shivering as heat curled low in my belly. If he could do that with just one look...

Oh God, I'm toast.

Our eyes met again, and I held my breath. Despite wanting him to make the first move, I lifted a hand in greeting. He smiled and returned my wave.

Never once breaking eye contact, he slipped out of the woman's grasp, said something to her, and grabbed two glasses from a passing tray. Without a backward glance, he headed straight for me, his long, casual stride eating up the distance between us.

The closer he got, his grin grew wider, making my pulse thump faster. He certainly didn't look like he had babysitting on his mind. In fact, it seemed the cat was about to catch the mouse, and I looked forward to letting him eat me.

Yes, please.

Practically salivating at the idea and a little too jittery, I slowed my breathing. In, then out, in rhythm with his steps. Almost here. This was it.

He stopped in front of me in all his sexy, magnificent godliness.

"Hello, luv." He leaned in to kiss my cheek and whispered, "Pretend to be my girlfriend."

"Your *what?*" My heart lurched as he straightened but remained close, too close, not close enough. I stared up at him, half tipsy but accepting the glass he handed me and half swooning at the heat of his words in my ear.

I'd heard him interviewed several times as the star wide receiver. His lilt, at the time, had been a lusty Texas drawl, mixed with the occasional slip into an oh-so sexy hint of British.

He'd explained once that he'd grown up in Dallas but spent summers with his "mum" in England. But now, he seemed to have lost a lot of his drawl, sounding more clipped, more English.

"Is she following me?" He indicated with a slight jut of his chin toward the woman he'd been talking to.

I sipped from the glass absent-mindedly, burning my two-glass rule to ashes. How could I say no when—

Wait. What had he just asked? My brain catching up with my ears, I cocked my head to one side to peek over his shoulder. Whoever the blonde was, she remained where he'd left her, though she certainly looked pissed. "No."

"Good." He took a drink of his champagne.

Was she his girlfriend and had he just dumped her? I almost felt sorry for the woman, but his request of pretense fit right into my plans.

Knowing I shouldn't, I tipped my glass to my mouth and emptied it, then blindly set it aside, not the least concerned that it rested next to a precious piece of art. I took his glass and placed it beside mine, then laid a hand on his chest and looked up at him from under my lashes. "What kind of girlfriend would you like me to be?"

He quirked a brow. "What are my options?"

"Well, there's the serious, clingy, totally in love girlfriend." I swiveled to his side and looped my arm through his as the blonde had done. Leaning into him, I laid my head on his shoulder as I pretended to study the painting. Yet I could only think about the hard grooves of his biceps under my hand, his purely masculine scent, and how to control my jagged breathing.

I let the moment last as long as possible, savoring his closeness, in case the next step in my plan failed, then said, "*Or...*"

I pivoted to stand in front of him again, closer than he'd allowed moments ago, my body flush against his from chest to thighs. My palms rested just under the lapels of his shirt. The heels I wore put my eyes even with his stubbled chin and my throbbing pussy against his lengthening dick.

Meeting his stormy gray eyes, I turned loose all the desire I'd felt for him as a teen. All the lust now dancing like flames in my core.

He blinked in surprise even as one hand settled on my waist, the other on my lower back to draw me tighter against him. Then his eyes darkened, and the hard length nestled perfectly at my center flexed. "*Or?*"

His reaction boosted my confidence. This was it, my first, last, and only chance to act on my fantasy of Michael Winters.

I shoved aside my insecurities and shifted one thigh, just enough to straddle his without being too blatant in the crowded room. Fingering the silky golden-brown hair at the back of his neck, I said, "I could be the girlfriend who's only in London to get lucky, and all I can think about is getting you alone and naked and fucking you until it's time to catch my flight home."

Michael

I HALF GRUNTED/HALF groaned as my dick thickened behind the fly of my trousers. What else could I say to the woman pouring herself over me like smooth whiskey over ice?

I brushed a finger along her cheek. "I'll go with getting lucky in London."

From the moment I caught this beauty boldly checking me out, my skin had zinged with a primal attraction, and I'd struggled to remember I was here to meet Dominic, Sarah, and— What was his sister's name? Rose? Lily? Some flower name.

When they'd failed to show, I'd enjoyed a flirtation with this stunning creature and ignored the chanting in my head—*no distraction, no distraction, no distraction.* Then bloody Liz had appeared, and my "no distraction" had become my savior.

And criminy, what a savior. Tall and

slender, with curves I wanted to explore with my fingers and then my tongue. The filmy black dress hugged her lithe frame, then flared as it ended near mid-thigh. And those legs...

I cleared the lust from my throat and smiled into her big brown, bedroom eyes. "I really could kiss you, right here, right now."

"Might help your cause." Her gaze fell to my mouth, blatantly inviting me to taste hers. Ignoring the voice of reason that reminded me this wasn't the place, I lowered my head.

"So this is your new flavor of the week?"

The venomous insult startled us both and broke the seductive spell I'd been under. I stepped back from the delight in my arms. I'd probably have to escort Liz outside to prevent a scene and give up the enchanting woman at my side. "Liz, look—"

"Yes, that would be me, this week's flavor." Looping her arm through mine, my charming rescuer pressed her breasts into my biceps. "But don't worry. I'm only in town to fuck him for a few days. You can have him back when I'm done."

I choked at the blatantly crude words coming out of her mouth and would have laughed if I'd been able to catch my breath.

Liz's eyes widened, and her mouth opened and closed several times, then clamped shut. The shock that matched mine wore off, and jealousy narrowed her eyes. "Crass American bitch."

A soft, feminine chuckle drifted over me, and the woman at my side placed a proprietary palm on my chest as she looked up at me. "I'd say she doesn't miss much, but she doesn't seem smart enough to realize you're done with her." She gave Liz a dismissive wave. "Move along. You're causing a scene."

Liz glanced around, and I followed suit. Several people were openly staring. Her spine stiffened, and she lifted her chin. "Please excuse me."

Nose in the air, Liz took her leave, but only to the other end of the gallery to join her friends.

I hated to hurt her, though she didn't really look as hurt as she did psychotic, glaring at me from behind one of her friends, making me wonder what I'd ever seen in her...other than her triple E tits.

I returned my attention to the woman clinging to me. "I'm sorry you had to be a party to that."

"No problem." She released my arm and faced the painting. Was it my imagination or was there a chill in her voice? Or was she bored now that the drama had passed? "So what's the story with Liz? She your ex?"

"Hardly." I studied the colors on the canvas with a frown. "Same old story. She wanted a relationship. I just wanted to have fun."

"Fun meaning sex."

Heat flooded my face, though I couldn't

imagine why her blunt assessment affected me that way. But I liked how she said what she wanted without apology. I'd forgotten that about women from the States. "Yes."

Her big brown eyes sliced my way, and lush red lips tipped upward in a sultry smile. "Fun is good."

Perhaps I'd mistaken the shift of her temperament. I returned her smile with a grin. "Fun can be *very* good."

"How long were you together?"

"A few days." And clearly, even that was too long. "And we weren't *together*. I met her on a trip to the country with friends, but when we got home, she wanted more. I didn't."

I'd tried to let Liz down easy, but the constant texts and phone calls and having her show up wherever I was made it difficult. Like tonight. It was as if she had a tracker on me.

I cast another glance across the room and found Liz still watching me. If it weren't for the mysterious woman at my side, I'd have left the exhibit by now.

Delicate fingers linking with mine drew my gaze. I glanced up from our hands to find curious dark eyes searching my face. "What?"

"She seems intent on ruining your evening."

I couldn't read her expression. Was she about to tell me she wanted no part of my drama? I wouldn't blame her. Our flirty beginning had spiraled. "And yours, I'm afraid."

"Only *you* could do that." She shook her

head for emphasis and teetered on her heels. I caught her against my chest, my hands on her upper arms. Those full breasts pressed against me, almost spilling from her dress.

My cock, which had deflated at the sound of Liz's voice, stirred to life again, and I thought I might do anything for a glimpse of the nipples hiding just out of sight. "How's that, luv?"

"Well," she purred, splaying her hands on my chest, "you made a choice, and I'm still waiting."

My gaze flew upward to meet hers. "For what?"

She smiled. "To get lucky."

Danielle

I BLINKED IN DISAPPOINTMENT as Michael scanned the gallery. I'd thought we were back to flirting, but instead of accepting my obvious invitation, he'd turned serious again. I felt as if I were on a roller-coaster of emotion. Or was that the champagne catching up with me?

Shouldn't have had that third glass.

What was he looking for anyway? A better question would be, *who* was he looking for? My brother? No, Dominic said he'd explained the situation and let Michael know I'd be alone, so—

Wait. Was he looking for a better offer? Did he regret dumping Skizzy Lizzy?

My tummy tumbled, but before I could tell him to forget it, his beautiful blue eyes, gleaming with lusty purpose, returned to mine.

His lips parted in a sexy grin. "Your place or mine?"

The acidic flare of jealousy that had simmered in my belly turned to smoldering flames of lust...and a bit of remorse for misjudging him. "Yours."

"Let's go." He grabbed my hand and led me through the maze of art and people. As we passed Dizzy Lizzy, I couldn't resist taunting the woman with a smug smile and a wave goodbye.

As soon as I stepped into the cool night air, the fog in my brain cleared, but only enough to make me wonder when I'd become such a bitch. Pride had always been my downfall, but petty jealousy?

I blamed the alcohol.

And tomorrow you'll blame your rash decision to sleep with Michael on it, too.

"Damn straight," I muttered under my breath and almost bumped into him when he stopped at the curb.

"There's one," he said as if I had a clue what *one* he referred to. His hand at my back as he guided me to a waiting taxi dissolved the guilt threatening to spoil my good time.

He opened the door, and I slid into the backseat. As he got in beside me, his thigh, hard and hot, grazed mine, and I shivered. He gave the driver an address in Kensington and settled back in the seat.

I couldn't wait any longer. I had to touch him. As I turned into him, he reached for me. Our breaths had only a second to mingle before his firm lips met mine. Too needy to be coy, I opened to him. His tongue swept me into a hot, hungry vortex of passion. I gripped his collar and tugged him closer.

A hand landed on my bare thigh, then tunneled beneath the hem of my dress. His other arm tightened around my back, mashing my breasts against his hard chest. His heat enveloped me, making me shudder again, and his fingers drove into the hair at the base of my skull and angled me into a deeper kiss.

My heart raced. My clit pulsed. I almost couldn't breathe. I didn't care.

The strong, athletic fingers on my thigh squeezed, dragging my hips toward him. My purse dug into my hip, denying the connection I most craved. With a garbled cry of frustration, I swung my leg over his thighs and rose to straddle him.

He groaned, and I whimpered as my pussy lined up with the long, thick ridge under his fly. The fingers under my dress had glided farther up and now gripped my hip to hold me still, preventing the grind I needed to fling me over the edge of orgasm.

His other hand fisted in her hair and tugged lightly. He slowed the kiss, then withdrew to nip at my lower lip. "Wait."

I opened my eyes but couldn't think for the stupor of unfulfilled need enthralling me. "Huh?"

He chuckled. "Let's slow down a bit."

Wait? Slow down? Michael Winters was finally kissing me, touching me, and about to do some downright nasty things to me. I'd waited over a decade for this. I didn't want to wait anymore. I didn't want to slow down. I wanted to fuck him.

And judging from the pulsing cock between my legs, *he* wanted to fuck *me*.

Well, his dick did. Maybe his brain didn't.

God, I'd done what I feared most when coming out tonight. I'd made a fool of myself, throwing myself at him like I'd seen the college girls do after his games. Social media had been full of videos with giggling females flashing their boobs at him.

Bile rose in my throat and my nose burned as moisture gathered in my eyes. I released my tight grasp on his hair and crawled off his lap. Shoving my dress back in place to cover my damp thighs, I faced the window. "I'm sorry."

"Don't be sorry." His hand fell to my thigh again, and he leaned closer to whisper, "I'm not. I love how hot you are right now, even as you sulk."

"I'm not—"

"And if you knew how badly I want to lay you down on this seat, drive balls deep, and make you come all over my dick, you'd know exactly how sorry I'm not."

Another shudder rippled through me. My nipples beaded, and my core clenched. A streak of pleasure zipped back and forth between the two. Though I'd been just as crude earlier, Michael's erotic words aroused me more than they should have. No one had ever said things like that to me. "Then why—"

"I don't think this fellow deserves a free show, and I'm too possessive to share a view of your sweet little ass with him." He leaned back in the seat but kept his hand on my leg, his index finger teasing circles on the inside of my knee. "Besides, we should introduce ourselves, don't you think?"

Huh?

"I'm Michael," he went on. "Michael Winters. I'm pleased to meet you..."

I whirled to face him, confusion slamming hard into my alcohol-ridden and lust-rattled brain. Had he really just introduced himself? Surely, he was kidding. But the patient anticipation on his face said he wasn't.

"And you are..." he prompted once more, confirming my thoughts as he released my thigh and swung his arm around my shoulders to draw me into his side. He nuzzled my ear with his nose.

"Danielle," I murmured.

There. Now, he would figure it out. After all, he'd been at the gallery to meet Dominic and Sarah and...*me.*

"Mmm, lovely name. It suits you." He kissed my neck, then looked at me. "And do you have a last name, Danielle?"

Nothing. No recognition in his eyes or voice. Then it dawned on me. He'd expected Dominic and Sarah and *Daisy.* He probably didn't know my real name.

I didn't know whether to laugh or to cry, par for the course of the evening. Finally, after years of dreaming about it, I'd garnered his notice. He wanted me. Yet he didn't. Not Daisy. He wanted Danielle, a stranger.

My gaze traveled over that firm jaw, lightly sprinkled with stubble. He watched me with hooded eyes. I couldn't fathom it. We'd flirted and exchanged sexually intoxicating innuendos, and the whole time I'd only been a random hookup to him.

What difference does it make? Any of it? The point is, he wants *me.*

And I want him even if he doesn't know who I am.

"You don't have a last name?" he teased.

Despite the turmoil raging in my head, I laughed, and tension eased from my muscles. I could work with this new situation, continue the game of fun and flirtation we'd started. I'd deal with the fallout tomorrow.

I laid a palm on his chest and fingered the crisp hair at the vee of his shirt. "A woman is allowed a few mysteries."

"I bet you have more than a few." The deep rumble of his voice soothed more of the jagged edges of my pride.

I tilted her head to one side and lifted a brow in challenge. "You're welcome to uncover as many as you dare."

With a groan, he scooted forward, the movement taking me with him. He tapped on the window between us and the cab driver. "Can you go a little faster?"

Chapter Three

Danielle

THE TAXI PULLED TO A STOP in front of a row of two-story flats. Michael opened the door, and I followed him out of the cab. I leaned into him as he paid the driver, not because I couldn't stand on my own. The dizzying effects of the champagne were wearing off, but I preferred his closeness.

One arm around me, he bustled me up the front steps and reached into his pocket. I turned into him, back against the door, my mouth seeking the skin beneath his stubbled jawline. I twined an arm around his neck. He'd teased me mercilessly in the cab, and the ride to his place had taken way too long.

"Let me unlock the door." He fumbled around me to insert the key as I slid a hand over his tented slacks. He grunted and tried to dodge my efforts to grip his cock. "Not fair."

I laughed. "As fair as your hand halfway up my skirt in the taxi?"

The key turned the lock, and a second later,

I staggered backward. Catching me, he walked me backward into the darkened entry and kept going until I hit the wall nearest the open door. My hip knocked against a small table, and I struggled for purchase, my feet tangling with something squishy.

He kicked whatever it was out of the way and slanted his mouth over mine. The heat in my core flared. The kiss was wild, frenzied, and stole my breath. He tasted so good, like champagne and mint. I couldn't get enough. Fantasy had nothing on the real Michael.

I was vaguely aware of the door shutting before he cupped my breast. Arching into him, I savored the heat of his palm. His other hand slipped under my dress and lifted my leg to wrap it around the back of his thigh. He ground his hips into mine. Need speared deep in my core as his hard erection rode against my clit.

We moaned as one, and he thrust again. A cry tore from my lips as a jolt of pleasure burst from my center, a sharp and explosive promise of things to come. And fuck, I wanted to come.

He eased out of the kiss, his mouth hovering a breath away as if ready to dive back in. "I can't wait."

"Please don't." I ran my fingers over his chest to the ripple of abs above his waistband. The ache to have him inside me had me searching for his belt.

His breathing labored, he opened some space as he trailed his lips to the crook of my neck and along my shoulder. "Hurry, luv."

With a giggle and a tug, I slipped the notch loose and undid the clasp of his pants. "Now, he says hurry."

A muffled chuckle tickled the flesh above my neckline where his lips teased. Warm fingers rose to loop around my bra strap and drag both it and my dress over my shoulder to the crook of my elbow, making it difficult to achieve my task. He yanked the cup down until my breast popped free. He palmed it, squeezed, and his tongue circled the nipple.

A current of delicious heat zipped from my breast to my pussy. "Oh, God."

The whir of his zipper joined the tearing sound of my panties. He yanked them off as if they were made of tissue rather than lace. Panting, I shoved his pants and boxers down. His cock, hot and heavy and silk over steel, fell into my palm. On instinct, my fingers curled around it.

"No." He grabbed my wrist and shackled it in a vise-like grip against the wall by my head, caging me. He lowered his forehead to mine. "One touch and I'm gone."

My heartbeat racing, I nipped at his lower lip and tilted my hips so that his dick slid between my folds and grazed my throbbing clit. Tendrils of heat snaked down my thighs, eliciting a gasp. "Condom. Now. Please."

He groaned and eased back, only to slide slowly back into place. "Upstairs."

"Seriously?" I didn't want to move. The spell might be broken, not to mention the loss of all those delicious feelings. I lifted my leg higher, hooking my knee on his hip and undulated to his slow rhythm. As his shaft rubbed my sensitive clit, I considered saying to hell with a condom, but this was Michael, and I was merely his flavor of the week.

"Afraid so." He started to pull away when I remembered the condom in her purse.

"Wait. I have one." I scrambled for the clutch bag and found it still hanging on the shoulder he hadn't undressed yet. Unsnapping the latch, I dug into the little zipper pocket and pulled out the neon yellow packet. "It's not mine. I was holding it for a friend."

"Sounds like something you tell your parents about the weed in your backpack." He took the condom and tore it open with his teeth. "But tell your friend I'm ever so grateful."

I watched him roll the rubber over the broad head and down the long shaft and couldn't help but laugh. My shoulders shook so hard my purse fell to the floor, its contents clattering around our feet.

"Any other time a woman laughed at my dick, I'd be offended, but..." He looked down at the neon yellow glow-in-the-dark condom with bold black letters along the shaft. It read, *Rip It, Grip It, Roll It, Dip It.*

"It's blinding me." Giggling, I could barely speak. Maybe the champagne hadn't worn off.

He swooped in to capture my lips. The spongy head of his cock tested my wet opening. I squirmed, trying to get him inside me. And then he drove deep, filling me with one thrust.

He drew his head back. "Bloody hell, you feel good."

"Back atcha."

The thickness of his erection stretched my inner walls, and the ridge around the tip teased my G-spot. Supported by his body and the wall, I lifted both legs to anchor them around his waist. He slipped deeper.

I moaned and drove my fingers into the hair at his nape to tug him closer. "Kiss me."

His lips grazed mine, then claimed them with the force of a hurricane that dragged me back into the storm of lust. The rhythm he set was hard and fast, his dick pounding into me. The friction spun me higher.

After dreaming of having Michael like this my entire adult life and aching for him since the moment Dominic said his name today, my orgasm built quickly. White-hot pleasure exploded from my core, threading down my thighs like molten lava. My toes curled. My pussy clenched around him, and my fists tightened in his hair, pulling as I cried out in his mouth.

Breaking the kiss, he threw back his head and plunged deep—one, two, three times—then stiffened as his release overtook him. Hot pulsing streams jetted into the condom and sent sizzling aftershocks along my nerve endings.

With the last spasm fading and reality slowly breaching the edges of euphoria, I clung to Michael, savoring the feel of his warm skin against mine, the light tickle of his chest hair against my nipples, the strength of his arms banded around me as if he would never let go, the intimacy of his cock still hard inside me. I wanted time to stop, for the fantasy to last forever.

But my limbs grew heavy, and I lost the battle. Arms dropping to my sides, I shivered as the heat of my body warred with the cool air we'd let in. Each breath was another battle to fight. God, he was everything I'd dreamed of and more.

He dropped his head onto my shoulder. "Bloody hell, you've wrung me dry."

Smiling, I lowered my legs until my toes touched the floor. He grunted but lifted his head and slowly pulled out. Stepping back, he tugged up his boxers and pants and tucked his cock, condom and all, behind the fly and zipped.

He caught me watching him and grinned. "Ready for round two?"

"Sounds great, but I can't move." My legs felt like rubber bands. If not for the wall, I'd be on the floor. Yet, somehow, I sagged deeper against the wall, relief washing over me. I'd half expected him to say thanks and call me a cab. But if he was up for more, I'd take it and whatever scraps he tossed my way. "I think I can manage to give us a head start, though."

As if he, too, had trouble standing, he shuffled backward a few feet into the shadowy living room and propped his ass against the back of the sofa. A beam of light sliced through a window, revealing a sexy grin that had me squeezing my thighs together. "How do you plan to do that, luv?"

"By removing any obstacles that might slow us down." With only a moment's hesitation, I grabbed the hem of my dress and lifted it up and over my head. I reached behind my back and fingered the hooks of my bra until they gave way. The urge to cover myself rose as the last of my armor fell to the floor. Instead, I unbuckled the strap on one heel and dropped it beside my dress. The other sandal joined its mate.

Wiggling my toes, I tilted my head and smiled. "Your turn."

Michael

I COULD ONLY DISTINGUISH the shadowy outline of Danielle's long, willowy body slumped against the wall. Darkness hid the parts she'd uncovered, making her even more mysterious.

Who was this woman?

From the moment I'd seen her, I was drawn to her. Sexually, yes. I'd never been so desperate to fuck a woman before, at least not since my teens. But she intrigued me on another level. One I couldn't fathom.

"Well?" she prompted, a hint of uncertainty behind the taunt.

I pushed off the back of the sofa and closed the distance between us. "Let's take this upstairs."

Snagging her hand, I tugged her against my chest, savoring the softness of her curves and the breathless gasp that escaped lips still swollen from my kisses. With a growl, I turned her to face the stairs and urged her up the first step before I fucked her against the wall again.

I started to follow, but my foot stalled on the first tread. The light from the transom window cast her in a warm glow. My mouth watered as I savored the sway of her ass. My dick flexed, reminding me I still wore the damn condom.

She made it to the fourth step and stopped to look over her shoulder. "Aren't you coming?"

"Not yet, but I will be," I muttered and then spoke up, "Right behind you, luv."

She trod up another step—the one that squeaked and I always told myself I'd fix—and stopped again when I didn't move. "Are you looking at my ass?"

"Absolutely." I chuckled. "Your ass and every lovely inch of you."

Boldly, she turned around to face me and posed in a way that said, *"Here I am. Look to your heart's content."*

I did just that, scanning from her wiggling toes, up her mile-long legs, one knee bent to modestly hide her feminine secrets, to the delicate hand resting on the stair rail, then past her full, high breasts to sultry brown eyes.

"Are you done?" she asked. "Have you had your fill?"

"Not even close."

"Well, you can look more later. Right now, you're too far away." She crooked a finger and backed up two more steps. Her playful naughtiness triggered mine.

Eyes locked with hers, I stalked slowly up the first few steps, then took the rest two at a time. She squealed and tried to escape, but I bent to catch her around the waist and hauled her over my shoulder.

I swatted her bare ass. "That's for teasing. My poor dick can't take it, you know."

A second later, my right butt cheek stung from the slap she returned. "And that's for ruining my fun."

"Don't you worry. You'll get all the fun you want, and then some."

"Mmm, fun is good."

I smiled as I entered my bedroom and flipped the wall switch. Light flooded the space. This time, when we had *fun*, I wanted to see her—all of her.

Stopping by the bed, I lowered her slowly, inch by inch, to the floor, enjoying the feel of her softness.

She peered up at me, her fingers releasing the top button of my shirt. "You are far too overdressed."

Her hair was a tidal wave of curls, mussed from hanging upside down. I swept it behind her ears, so I could study her face as she concentrated on the task. "Where are you from? I know the U.S., but what area?"

Her fingers stilled on the last button, and she looked up at me again. "New York. Why?"

I shrugged and toed off my shoes. "I thought I heard a hint of the Southern states."

She opened the last button and shoved the shirt over my shoulders and down my arms. Her hands glided back up, exploring as they traversed over the curves of my biceps and the corner of my shoulder.

Closing my eyes, I gave her the wheel, enjoying her touch. "I lived in Texas while I was growing up."

Her hands stilled for a moment, then meandered over my pecs, pausing to flick my nipples with her fingernail, then moving onward to the waistband of my pants. My belt was still undone, along with the top button of my trousers, so she made quick work of the zipper.

"I miss it sometimes." I wasn't sure why I was telling her all this, why I was talking at all, or why I felt it was important for her to know.

I opened my eyes and glanced at the pinkened flush of her cheeks, the thick black lashes that fanned her high cheekbones, and puffy rose-hued lips. A mystery but a beautiful one.

Lowering my head, I brushed my lips against the hair at her temple.

A sweet, subtle fragrance filled my nostrils. "You smell so good. Like honey."

"I condition with it sometimes." Her teeth grabbed one corner of her lower lip as she dragged my pants over my hips, then knelt to push them all the way down to pool around my ankles.

"There, that's—" Her gaze locked on my dick, and a trickle of melodic laughter rushed up at me. "I can't talk to you with that ridiculous thing on your..." She waved a hand at the yellow condom still adorning my dick.

"Hey, this ridiculous thing saved the day a few minutes ago." I stepped out of my pants and boxers, then hurried to the bathroom.

After quickly disposing of the *ridiculous* condom, I washed up. When I returned to the bedroom, I was disappointed to find her lying on the bed on her side facing away from me, her long legs bent slightly, her dark hair spread across the gray duvet. I'd hoped she'd still be kneeling, and I'd have those full lips wrapped around my dick.

She twisted to look at me. "That's much better."

Needing to touch her, I grabbed her ankle and turned all the way over. Eyes half-shuttered, she propped herself on one elbow and crooked a finger at me like she'd done on the stairs. Her pink tongue slipped over her bottom lip to wet its fullness.

My cock bounced toward my abs as if to say, *"Do what she says, dumbass."*

I massaged her foot, finding the erogenous pressure point. "Before we go any further, I have to know. How did you come by a glow-in-the-dark condom?"

She settled on both elbows and grinned. "I was with some friends in New Orleans for Mardi Gras two years ago. One of the parade floats threw condoms instead of necklaces. Kate caught one but didn't have anywhere to put it, so I stashed it in my purse and forgot it was in there until I tried to pay for my cab with it earlier tonight."

"I'll bet the driver loved that."

"You have no idea." Lying back, she stretched her arms over her head. "Now, are you going to talk all night or take care of business?"

"Oh, luv," I said, placing one knee on the bed and lifting her foot to kiss each toe, "this is anything but business. And if my options are to look at your lovely body or bury myself in that lovely pussy, I'm happy to do either. Both are quite pleasurable."

"You are a sweet talker, aren't you? And you love your options."

"I love *your* options." I waved my free hand to encompass her body.

She slid a hand to her breast and cupped it. "Then let me help you decide which option needs your attention." Her thumb and forefinger pinched the rosy bud and twisted. "There are my nipples..." Keeping the pinch/twist action going, she trailed the fingers of her other hand between her breasts, down the contours of her belly to the hill of her pubic bone. Her middle finger plowed the strip of dark curls and glided through pink, glistening folds. "And there's..."

Fuck, she was hot...and beautiful...and obviously smart...and funny...and fucking hot.

With a growl, I drew her foot out to one side to expose the little swollen kernel she worked in circles, mesmerizing me. "You are the most divine creature."

Her parted lips curled upward, and her teeth caught the bottom one as she arched her back and moaned.

I needed to see more.

Grasping her other ankle, I pushed her legs up and wide and planted her feet on the mattress near her ass, then let gravity and her relaxed state open them for my viewing pleasure. I stood back, my dick in hand, to watch this amazing woman masturbate. I pumped my fist in time with the circles she made around her clit.

Imagining it was her tongue, I swirled my thumb through the slick fluid seeping from the head of my cock, then over and around the sensitive ridge. A growl rumbled from my throat as heat centered in my balls.

Her eyelashes fluttered and opened, her sultry dark eyes revealing the lust coiling inside her. She zeroed in on my hand stroking my erection.

"That is so hot," she breathed.

"*You* are hot." I grabbed a condom from the nightstand, ripped it open with my teeth, and stopped stroking long enough to roll it on. "And I really need to be inside you."

It was no lie. No woman had ever made me this eager, this desperate. But somehow, tonight, my need was about Danielle. As if not having her would be painful, not only physically but emotionally, which confused me more than it scared me.

But my brain wasn't in control at the moment, and my dick didn't give a good god damn about analyzing my bloody musings.

Crawling up her body, I skimmed her smooth, tanned legs with my fingertips. *Like velvet.* I wanted to stop when I reached her pussy, aching to taste her, but I needed inside her more.

I captured both her wrists, putting a halt to her self-pleasuring. A small whimper escaped her, making my balls tighten. I sucked her glistening fingers into my mouth and groaned as her tangy essence hit my tastebuds. "Mmm, sweet. I'll have more of that later."

Settling into the cradle of her hips, my weight on my elbows, I pressed both her hands to the mattress beside her head. Watching her expression, I nudged the head of my cock to her slick entrance and flexed my hips.

I slid in an inch and sighed. Hot. Tight. Heaven.

"More," she murmured.

I wanted to slam deep, but more than that, I wanted to take my time this round. To feel her pussy grip me tighter and tighter. To see her face when I made her come apart. To make the best sex I'd ever had last longer than it had downstairs.

Giving her what she'd asked for—no, demanded—I rocked my hips, screwing deeper and deeper until I sank balls-deep. Lacing my fingers with hers, I lowered my mouth to eat at her lips in leisurely licks, bites, and hungry kisses as I fucked her with slow rolling thrusts.

Feet still planted on the mattress, she rose to meet me, seemingly satisfied with the pace I set, but her nails dug into my ass as she tried to force me deeper. Pain merged with pleasure, and fuck, she did something with her inner muscles on the slide back in that made my head spin.

I ripped my mouth from hers. "Bloody hell, luv, you feel exquisite."

"Danielle," she whispered between quick shallow breaths. "My name...is Danielle."

"Danielle," I ground out and hooked my

elbow under her knee to change the angle.

"Aaaahh, yes, fuck, yes!" She arched, her hips locked, as I pistoned in and out, driving her through the orgasm gripping my cock. Little mewling sounds distorted by the loud hammering of blood in my ears had me plunging harder, faster. Tears leaked from her eyes, but I couldn't stop.

A tingling at my spine signaled my release. I tried to hold back, but that would have been like trying to catch a tidal wave in a bucket. My balls tightened, and I gave a guttural shout as hot spurts of cum shot through my shaft and into the condom. Waves of sweet bliss rushed over me with the power of a tsunami.

Long minutes passed before I was able to breathe normally. My arms quaked with the need to collapse, but I managed to untangle my fingers from hers and gently thumbed the next tear racing toward her hairline. My gut twisted with guilt. "I'm sorry, luv."

"Don't be sorry, and don't call me luv." She sniffed and lifted wet lashes to peer up at me, the softness of her deep brown eyes warming me in ways that had nothing to do with sex. "That was the most...beautiful orgasm I've ever had."

"So these are good tears?" I held my breath.

"Oh, yeah."

I brushed a kiss across her lips and smiled. "It was pretty spectacular, wasn't it?"

She sniffed again and pushed playfully at my shoulder. "Look who's getting a big head."

Reluctantly, I eased off her and slipped out of bed to get rid of the condom encasing my reemerging hard-on. I wanted her again.

When I returned to the bedroom, she was back on her side, this time facing me, and she was asleep on top of the bedding, one arm under her head. The other hand tucked under her cheek. I hated to wake her, but I gently shifted her to one side to pull the sheet and comforter down.

"Just five more minutes," she grumbled when I rolled her the other way and pulled the covers over her.

Chuckling, I crossed the room and turned off the light. Laughter seemed to go hand in hand with this woman. And it felt damn good. A yawn dragged me back to the bed to crawl in behind her, spoon fashioned.

She squirmed closer, clutching my arm. I kissed her hair, tightened my arm around her, and closed my eyes. I couldn't remember the last time I'd snuggled with a woman after sex...if ever. But I'd be damned if I could let go of this one.

One thing was abundantly clear, and this I could admit. Danielle was not just another distraction. She was so much more.

Chapter Four

Michael

I WOKE TO THE WARMTH of a soft, pliable body next to me. My morning wood had me seeking out her comfort. She grumbled when I made contact, and I opened my eyes. *Danielle.*

She lay on her side, her face half buried in a pillow with dark brown waves hiding the other half. One knee was bent. The sheet rested on the swell of her hip, leaving full, creamy breasts on display.

Propping on one elbow, I trailed my fingers over her shoulder, dragging kisses behind them, down the back of her ribs to her waist. We hadn't had sex again after going to sleep, despite my plans to spend all night fucking her into oblivion. I flexed my hips so that she'd feel how hard I was.

With an unintelligible whine, she scooted away and shoved her head under the pillow. Obviously not a morning person.

Smiling at her grumpiness, I rolled the other way and swung my legs over the edge of the bed. As I made my way to the bathroom to shower, I shook my head over the fact that I was happy to let her sleep. Usually, I'd be eager to get my bed partner on her way and uncomfortable if she lingered too long. But I didn't want Danielle to leave. I wanted more time to explore the feelings she evoked in me.

My mother had always said, "You'll know when you know."

All my life I'd listened to my gut. My instinct had never led me wrong, whether it was reading a route on the football field and knowing when to change the play or getting the sense of a client and what they wanted before they themselves knew. And I knew almost instantly when a woman wasn't the right one for me.

But something deep inside told me this woman might be different.

After I showered and dressed in jeans and a T-shirt, I grabbed my phone and trotted downstairs. As I hit the fifth tread from the bottom, it squeaked, reminding me of our game on the stairs last night. I grinned, a bounce in my step as I entered the kitchen.

A few minutes later, I had coffee made and eggs whipped and scrambling in the pan. Setting the spatula aside, I poured a mug of the strong black brew and blew on it. Coffee was the only Americanism I couldn't give up when I'd made the move to England. Even after ten years, I simply couldn't abide tea.

Settling a hip against the counter, I called the office.

Jaycee picked up. "Good morning, Townes & Winters Design."

"Jaycee, it's Michael."

"Good morning, Mr. Winters."

"Good morning. Can you please tell Robert I won't be in today? I don't have any appointments, and something has come up."

"Of course."

"Cheers." I disconnected the call and scrolled through texts. There was one from my mother saying she hoped I had a good time last night. *If she only knew.*

A text alert went off as I was about to set aside my phone to tend the eggs.

Dom: *Sorry I didn't let you know we wouldn't be at the art exhibit. Daisy said she was too tired to go, and I'm with Sarah in South Africa. Her father is in ICU in Cape Town. Don't know when I'll be home. Daisy is at my apartment. Will you check on her? She hasn't answered any of my texts or calls.*

Daisy. *Yep, a flower.*

I thumbed a quick answer and made a mental note to follow through.

Me: *Sure. I'll run by your place at lunch.*

Tucking my phone in my back pocket, I

stirred the eggs and popped two slices of bread into the toaster. I planned to take Danielle to my favorite bistro near Portobello Road Market tonight. Then we could shop, eat, and stroll through Hyde Park. I don't know why it was important to me that she loved my city as much as I did.

Probably because I'd waited so long to find a woman who made me feel the way she did, and she would only be in England for a few more days. Wasn't that what she said? *Only in London to get lucky, and all I can think about is getting you alone and naked and fucking you until it's time to catch my flight home.*

Maybe I'd throw those words back at her and suggest she keep her word because just thinking about never seeing her again—

A squeak on the stairs told me that my sleeping beauty was finally awake. "I'm in the kitchen, luv." When she didn't answer, I called out, "Danielle?"

Still no answer.

I turned off the heat, laid the spatula on the spoon rest, and walked around the wall blocking my view of the living room. Wearing only the white dress shirt I'd worn the night before, Danielle was on her hands and knees, crouched low and looking under the sofa. Twin half-moons of creamy flesh peeked from the tailored hem.

My dick stretched toward my abs. I could take her from behind. Right there on the floor.

Or...she was already on her knees. It wouldn't—

"Damn it." The curse was barely audible, but the level of distress behind it broke into my lust-filled musings.

"Can I help?" I asked, striding toward her with every intention of forgetting breakfast and taking her back to bed as soon as she found what she was looking for.

She spun around, her hair wild, her dark eyes wide. Pink stained her cheeks and flowed down her neck. Slender fingers clutched her tiny purse to her chest. "I, um, I can't find the keys."

"What keys?"

"The ones to get back into D—the place where I'm staying." She crossed to the wall I'd fucked her against, dropped to her knees, and began stuffing things into the purse—a phone, a tube of lipstick, and a credit card.

"We'll find them later," I said, giving up on going back to bed for now. She didn't look like her morning grumps had worn off yet. "Come have breakfast. Do you drink coffee?"

Her head jerked up, and she shoved her hair out of her face. "I don't have time for coffee. I have to find those keys. I have a meeting at one."

Disappointment filtered into my hopes of having her all to myself today, but I rallied. Surely, whatever meeting she had planned wouldn't take long. My plans could work around hers. "Let me help you look."

She swiped her dress off the floor and held

out a hand to stop me in my tracks. "Turn around." When I didn't catch on, she added," So I can get dressed."

"You're kidding, right?" I laughed. "I've already seen you naked."

"That was last night." She waved a hand. "Hurry."

I did as she requested, no matter how silly. Material swished, presumably as my shirt came off, then swished again as her dress replaced it. How could the confident woman who stripped for me and masturbated while I watched turn into this shy and fidgety female?

I turned back around to find her flinging cushions from my couch. "I doubt they'd be there, luv. We never made it to the couch."

"Stop calling me luv and help me find them." She deserted the sofa to rifle through the peat moss covering the soil in a potted plant.

Not daring to point out the plant was across the room, I put in a serious effort to help her find her keys.

Ten minutes later, I heard a sniffle and dropped the curtain I'd just checked under. She was leaning against my now-favorite wall and wiping a tear from her cheek with the back of her hand.

Rising from my knees, I said, "Where is your meeting?"

"Downtown."

"Not to worry. I can take you."

She blinked at me and another tear fell,

only to meet its demise with another swipe. "I'm not worried about how to get there." She laughed. "But I can't go like this."

I took in her long legs and the swell of her breasts threatening to spill from the bodice of her rumpled dress. I agreed but went with humor. "I don't know why not." I grinned. "You've got my attention."

"Well, that's great"—she flung out her arms—"but I'm not trying to fuck the people I'm meeting, am I?" Her head fell back as regret washed over her face. "I'm sorry. That was a bitchy thing to say."

I let her words roll off my back. "No, I'm the one who's sorry. I shouldn't make light of a situation that clearly has you upset."

She slid to the floor, drew her knees to her chest, and wrapped her arms around them. Her forehead dropped to her knees. "This has all been a big mistake. I shouldn't be here."

Now, those words were different. Here I was thinking she might be the woman I'd been waiting for, and she called what we shared a mistake.

Oblivious to my thoughts, she went on, her voice muffled. "I'm sorry. I know guys like you are one and done. I wanted to be out of here before you woke up, but I overslept. And now, it's all awkward—" Another sniffle. "—and so fucking humiliating."

Guys like me? The words stung, but clearly, she wasn't wrong in her perception of me. Until last night, I'd been exactly the guy she described.

I crossed the space between us, sat beside her, my back to the wall, and pulled her onto my lap. She didn't fight me. Instead, she curled her arms around me and buried her face in my neck.

"Look at me, luv."

"Danielle," she murmured, her breath warming my skin.

"Danielle." I splayed a hand on the side of her face and used my thumb to tip her head back until her watery eyes met mine. "The only thing awkward is knowing you planned on sneaking out of here this morning without saying anything when *I* took the day off to spend more time with you."

Her eyes flared in surprise. "You did?"

"I did." I wiped the last of the wetness from her cheek. "And I have an idea that could solve your problem."

"A locksmith?"

Chuckling, I moved her from my lap, stood, and held out my hand. "No, we'll save that as a last resort."

She accepted my hand, and I pulled her to her feet. I couldn't resist the taste of her lips, but I kept it chaste. "You go shower, and I'll make a call."

Her brows dove into a doubtful frown, but she turned around and started up the stairs.

I headed for the kitchen, grabbed my coffee mug in one hand, and leaned against the island.

I pulled my phone from my pocket and pressed a number on speed dial, then lifted the mug to my lips. I took a gulp only to wince as I swallowed the tepid coffee.

I poured the rest in the sink as my mother answered, "Michael?"

"Hi, Mum."

"Are you all right?"

"Yes, but I need a favor for a friend." Until I figured out what this thing was with Danielle, *friend* was all my mother needed to know.

"What friend?"

"Her name is Danielle."

"Michael Chandler Winters, you haven't gotten this girl in trouble have you?"

I laughed. "No, Mum, it's nothing like that."

"I'm listening."

"Well, you see…"

Danielle

FEELING CLEAN AND somewhat calmer, I followed Michael to his car parked in front of his house. He said he could help me, so I had little choice but to put my fate in his hands.

"It's just a couple of blocks." He opened the

passenger door. "Normally, I would walk, but since we're in a bit of a time crunch…"

I slid into the sleek black sedan, and he shut the door. As he rounded the front of the car, I looked at him fully for the first time that morning. In jeans that hugged his ass and a T-shirt that had seen better days, he still sent a swarm of butterflies fluttering around in my belly.

How could anyone regret a night with this man? I certainly didn't. Not the night anyway. But I'd turned into a burden. He'd tried to assure me otherwise, that he wanted to spend the day with me, which thrilled the hell out of me. I just hoped it wasn't a mistake. I mean really, my fantasy had been fulfilled.

And yet, as he slid into the car with a happy grin and pulled away from the curb, the engine wasn't the only thing revved up and ready to go.

Michael wasn't lying. The trip literally took two minutes. He turned two corners and parked on a street similar to his. The front doors of the white homes were fewer and farther apart, indicating the homes were likely larger. Posher, too, judging by the architecture. This was old money England.

He jumped out of the car and hurried around to open my door while I was still gawking at the ornate beauty of the buildings.

"Who lives here?" I accepted his hand and unfolded from the comfy leather seats. If he'd brought me to one of his supermodel-thin booty calls, I was out of here, even if I had to walk all the way back to Chelsea.

The front door opened before he could answer, and a lovely woman in her fifties smiled serenely at us. Her hair was blonde with a hint of gray, her eyes were the color of thunder clouds, and she appeared to be about my height. The same build as me, too.

He greeted the woman with a kiss on the cheek. "Good morning, Mum."

Mum?

"Hello, darling." His mother glanced at me, never batting an eye. "Hi, I'm Laura."

"Danielle," I choked out.

"Come in, come in." She backed into the hall, so that we could enter, and Michael closed the door.

Her gaze swept over me, taking in the wrinkled dress, the amount of leg showing beneath the short hem, my hooker heels, and no makeup. This was not how I would have wanted to meet his mother, looking like a hot mess, not that I'd ever considered meeting her when years ago, Dominic had sung her praises.

"I understand we have a bit of a dilemma," his mother said.

I resisted the urge to tug on my dress. It wasn't going to get any longer. Instead, I smiled. "A bit of one, yes."

Laura looked at her son and nodded, then turned to lead the way into the living room. "I believe I have just what you need."

I grabbed Michael's arm to keep him in the entryway. "Your *mum*?" I whispered. "Really? You brought your one-night stand to your mother's house?"

This was no walk of shame. This was a fucking marathon.

He frowned, and his eyes flashed with... What? Anger? Hurt? Confusion? Whatever it was, it disappeared as he patted my hand and pulled me forward. "She's good at this. Trust me."

Feeling like a peasant, I let him drag me farther into the elegant home.

"Can I offer you something to drink?" his mother asked.

I didn't want to sound ungrateful, but—

"We're in a rush, Mum." Michael laced his fingers with mine. "Her meeting is at one."

"Then let's get to it, shall we?" Laura nodded as if to answer her own question, then looked at Michael. "Why don't you go find something to do and leave us to it?"

"Of course." He nudged me as his mother glided toward the stairs.

I balked. "Don't you dare leave me here."

"You'll be fine." His lips cut off my argument with a quick peck. "I'll go look for your keys again."

Then he was gone, and I stood staring after him.

"This way, dear."

Like a prisoner on my way to the gallows, I

followed Laura up the stairs and down a hall to an open door. I entered a bedroom decorated with whites and creams and tans. The only color was a painting with splashes of teal and blush pink. I wanted to explore it further, examine the brush strokes, to see who the artist was, but I contained my curiosity as Laura waved a hand toward the bed.

"I've taken the liberty of choosing a few possibilities," she said, "though Michael only explained it was for a meeting. If none of these are appropriate, we'll find something else, but he described you perfectly, so they should fit. We're about the same size."

Glancing from the clothes laid out on the bed to Laura, I struggled not to fidget. "I'm so sorry to have intruded on you this way."

"Nonsense. It's been a long time since my son has needed me. A mother misses that, you know."

Memories of my mother would argue that statement, but I read understanding in the woman's eyes. She wasn't judging. She was trying to help her son.

"Besides," Laura said, "when he said he was bringing over a girl, I admit I was a little excited and quite a bit curious. He's never brought a woman home to meet me."

And he still hasn't. But I couldn't tell this kind woman that her son was only taking pity on me because I'd bawled like a baby. I wasn't special to him, and I'd be gone by Monday.

"Well, I thank you all the same."

She nodded. "I'll put the kettle on while you try these on. I've left the rudimentary essentials of makeup"—she pointed to the vanity by the window—"though I dare say you don't appear to need much—if any."

Laura exited the room and closed the door behind her.

I stood there, overwhelmed by the generosity of both son and mother. My pride needled me to graciously decline their help, but unless Michael found Dominic's keys, I had no other choice. And saying no would be rude at this point.

Sighing, I removed my sad, wrinkled dress, which left me standing in the middle of the room in my bra and heels. Crossing to the bed, I carefully fingered the edge of a black jacket in one of the garment bags. It was lightweight wool, lined with black silk. The pants had a lean silhouette with fitted hips and a flare at the hem. This had to be designer.

I flipped the waistband of the pants and read the couturière's label. Lady Laura Chandler.

"Oh. My. God." How could I not have put it together? Michael's mother was *the* Lady Laura, one of my favorite fashion designers and far beyond my department-store budget. I couldn't afford the pants, much less the matching jacket. Still, I couldn't resist trying them on.

Slipping out of my heels, I stepped into the

pants and could honestly say I'd never felt such luxury. The lining was cool and soft against my bare legs, not to mention on my ass and lady bits. The white, silk shell went on next, a stark contrast against the ebony jacket with one button that nipped in at the waist. I slid back into my heels and turned to face the mirror. My legs looked longer than ever.

Wow! It was amazing what a well-tailored outfit could do for a woman's figure...and her ego. It was perfect, definitely a power suit.

I turned this way and that. So maybe I could splurge just a little. I could probably recoup the loss in...oh, say a year...and only if I got the new job.

A giggle escaped to fill the silence of the room. Dominic had offered to let me stay with him until I found an affordable alternative, but a year might be pushing it, especially with Sarah in the picture.

Without trying on the other beautiful piece's, I quickly took off the suit and blouse and hung them on a hook behind the door. Sitting at the vanity, I peered in the mirror and got to work pinning my hair in a loose-but-tidy, messy bun. A contradiction in terms if ever there was one.

Twenty minutes later, I gathered my torn dress and made my way to the stairs. Pausing at the top, I realized I had missed the neatly arranged grouping of pictures displayed on the staircase wall. One by one, I stopped to admire them. Michael as a boy of ten in a prep school uniform with his tawny hair and straight white smile. No doubt he'd broken many a little girls' hearts.

On the last step, I lingered to admire a couple of photos of him in his football uniform. One was with Dominic at the stadium after a game. The other was with his mother. His hair was a gorgeous mess, sweat plastering the front to his forehead, and his smile was infectious. My lips tilted upward, and I heaved a wistful sigh.

Dominic had said Michael's mother never missed a game, spent the entire fall season in the States just to watch him. That was when I had started saving to go see Dominic play. If Michael's mom could fly all that way from the UK—

"Here you are."

Startled, and feeling a little guilty for ogling her son, I took the last step down and smiled. "Just going down memory lane."

"Do you miss your family?" Laura asked, her head cocked to one side.

I blinked. *Fuck, did she catch my slip.*

Michael didn't know who I was, so why would his mother? "Oh, yes. I'm hoping to be closer to my family soon."

"Michael called. He's on his way," she said, without a trace of suspicion. "We'll have a nice chat and a cup of tea while we wait."

Following her to the kitchen, my conscience prickled. This woman was so kind, so...everything my mother had never been, and all I wanted to do was confess who I was, why I'd lied, and ask for advice.

Instead, I deviated from all talk of family. "The suit is lovely. You're very talented and one of my favorite designers."

"You're sweet." She stopped at the counter to pour us both a cup of tea and smiled, conspiratorially. "I was hoping you'd pick that one. From the moment I saw you, I knew it was perfect for you."

"I don't know how I'll ever pay you back for your help, but I will send payment for the suit."

Laura waved a hand in dismissal. "Nonsense. You look lovely in it. Besides, just seeing the look on my son's face when he looks at you is payment enough."

More guilt. How could I tell her she had it all wrong?

"How did you two meet? Are you a client?"

I sipped at her tea, stalling while I tried to figure out how to answer. I couldn't lie to her any more than I already had, after the kindness she'd shown. "We met through a friend."

Not a lie. Dominic was my brother, but he was also my best friend.

The front door opened and shut, and a second later, Michael joined us in the kitchen. His eyes widened, then sparked in appreciation...and hunger, which was entirely inappropriate with his mother standing there. "You look stunning."

His mother gave me an I-told-you-so nudge. Flushing from head to toe, I slid a glance to the woman whose eyes twinkled knowingly.

I lowered my cup to the counter. "I should go, but if you won't let me pay, I'll make sure this gets cleaned and returned to you as soon as possible."

"No need." Laura laid a hand on mine. "Think of it as a gift."

"I couldn't."

Michael moved in beside me and took my hand from his mother's grip. "You can't argue with my mum. She'll have her way no matter what." He turned to his mother. "Cheers, Mum. I owe you one."

He hurried me out the door and to the car. "We should have just enough time to get you there."

When he climbed into the driver's side, I leaned toward him and kissed his cheek. "Thank you."

He snorted as he started the car and gave me a sly grin. "I was expecting better recompense than that for coming to your rescue, but I'll seek payment later."

"Some knight in shining armor you are, wanting payment from a damsel in distress. What ever happened to chivalry?" I relaxed as he pulled into the lane and aimed for Central London. It was all working out, thanks to Michael and his mother. "I didn't know your mother was Lady Laura Chandler."

He slid me a quizzical smirk. "How could you?"

Fuck. "I-I just mean I'm surprised. That's all. The names don't match."

"She took back her maiden name when she divorced my father." His bitter tone told me I'd hit a nerve, so I changed the subject.

"She asked if I was a client. Do you often sleep with your clients?"

He chuckled. "No. But if you're fishing, I'm a partner in an architectural firm. In fact, my office isn't far from where you're meeting, so I might run by to pick up plans for a new client, and I have another errand to run."

When he didn't elaborate, I turned to look out the window and tried not to feel like shit for keeping secrets from him. He was so open and honest. I really needed to tell him I was Dominic's little sister and our meeting wasn't by chance. But the words wouldn't come, and I wasn't ready to end the fantasy or risk rejection. Not yet.

Twenty minutes later, he stopped in front of the fake address I'd given him. I wasn't sure if he knew Daisy's interview was with the museum, so I'd found a place close by. I'd have to catch a taxi or hoof it to my destination.

Before I could open the car door, he leaned over, his hand at the back of my neck, and pulled me in for a soul-searing kiss. My nipples peaked, and my core contracted. I melted into him just as he retreated.

His breath warmed her lips. "Now, that made all the hard work of your rescue worthwhile."

I shoved at his shoulder, giggling like a giddy teenager, and opened the door. "I have to go."

Once the door was shut behind me and I stepped onto the curb, the window rolled down. I ducked to look at him.

"I'll be right here waiting," he said, "when you're finished."

"Are you sure?" I figured I'd take a taxi to his place, find Dominic's keys, and make a graceful exit...if that was what he wanted. "I don't know how long I'll be."

"Doesn't matter." He waved and drove away.

As soon as Michael was out of sight, I hailed a cab and climbed in. Ten minutes later, I sat in the outer office at the back of the museum, trying to catch my breath. I ended up being five minutes early for my interview and took a moment to check my phone.

There were thirteen texts from Dominic. The first told me that he and Sarah had landed and were on the way to the hospital. The second was several hours later with news that Sarah's father was stable but still in ICU.

Worry showed up in the third.

Dominic: *Hey, text me back to let me know you're okay.*

Dominic: *Daize?*

Dominic: *Are you okay?*

Dominic: *Answer your phone.*

Dominic: *You're really scaring me.*

Dominic: *Dammit, Daisy. Where are you?*

His messages went on like that until the last one, which had come in five minutes ago.

Dominic: *If I don't hear from you in the next thirty minutes, I'm calling the police and catching a flight home.*

I looked up at the director's door to make sure I had time to answer. I couldn't let Dominic come home because I'd silenced my phone at the art exhibit last night and forgot to turn it back on because I was too busy having sex with his friend.

I thumbed as fast as I could.

Me: *Sorry. I'm fine. I was just tired last night, so I turned off my phone. I'm about to go into my interview. Love you!*

Lies, lies, lies. But there was no way I'd tell him the truth, that I'd seduced and slept with Michael. I could barely believe it myself.

Chapter Five

Michael

I RANG THE DOORBELL at Dom's house for the third time, then resorted to knocking—or rather banging—on the door. Still no answer.

Fishing out my phone, I texted Dom.

Me: *I'm at your place. No answer. Do you want me to call for a welfare check?*

I wasn't sure how long it would take for Dom to answer since he was likely taking care of Sarah, but the sky looked like it was about to open up, so I returned to my car for the wait. So much for taking Danielle sightseeing.

Glaring at the door as if I could summon Dom's sister, I tried to remember her but couldn't pull up an image. I'd only met her once...I think. Still, I couldn't not be a touch worried about her. She was alone in a strange country.

Of course, I had no idea if the girl had friends here or not. She could be out with one of them now.

"Typical teenager." If she wasn't in danger or hurt, the least she could do was respond to Dom's texts and calls. Not doing so was rather thoughtless. Not to mention the time I was taking from my limited time with Danielle. Granted, Danielle was in a meeting.

It dawned on me that I had no idea how long she'd be in London. She'd said a few days. I'd have to make it a point to find out when I picked her up.

My phone pinged.

Dom: *I just heard from her. She's fine. She turned off her phone and went to bed early. She's at the museum.*

Me: *OK, I'll check on her later. Text me her number so I can make sure she's expecting me.*

The number came through, and I tucked my phone onto the mount. I'd call her after I picked up Danielle.

Half an hour later, I parked twenty feet down the street so I could see her as she exited the building. Rain pelted the windshield, but I'd found my umbrella—or brolly as my mother called it—and I planned to catch Danielle before she was soaked. I should have asked for her number or given her mine, so she could text me when she was finished.

Keeping an eye on the door, I was startled

when the passenger door opened. Danielle slid onto the seat and quickly closed the door.

"I can't believe this rain." She reached for her dress in the backseat and mopped the rivulets running down her face. Her hair was plastered to her head, the little bun in the back sagging sadly. "I just hope your mom's suit isn't ruined."

"Where did you come from?" I turned the thermostat up to keep her from catching a chill and held up the umbrella. "I was watching for you."

"Oh, sorry." Rubbing her hands together, she leaned closer to the vents, her teeth chattering. "I finished early, so I was checking out that little shop across the way."

Nodding, I took her hands in mine and held them to my mouth to warm them with my breath. "I need to get you home so you can dry out. I'm afraid the storm has put a damper on our plans for this afternoon."

Leaning over the console, she huddled closer and smiled through a shiver. "I'll bet you can think of all kinds of *fun* to warm me up."

That was all it took to get my mind off everything except getting her back to my place and getting her naked. I put the car in drive and pulled into traffic. She tugged her hair from the bun, shook it out, and gravitated to the vents again.

"How did your meeting go?" I asked before I did something stupid, like pulling into the nearest parking lot and dragging her across the seat to ride my dick.

She looked out the passenger window. "I think it went well. How about yours? Your errand, I mean."

"All done, except I didn't get to go by my office."

"Don't let me get in the way of your work. I can wait in the car."

"There's nothing that can't wait." Now, to get to the question I really wanted to ask. "Is all your business in London done?"

Turning to look at me, she asked, "Yes, why?"

I stopped at a traffic light and met her wary expression. "You said you were only in London for a few days. Last night, at the exhibit? I just wondered how many is a few?"

"I fly home Sunday." Her eyes grew big. "Oh my God. I can't leave if I can't find those keys. My passport is in my suitcase."

"Don't worry, luv. We'll find them." Though I hadn't really put that much effort into it, I almost wished they couldn't be found.

"Danielle," she said, her lips thinning.

The light changed, but I had to wait for the car in front of me to move. Easing forward, I darted a glance at her. "Can I ask why you don't like it when I call you luv? It's a term of endearment. You know I don't mean anything sexually derogatory or condescending by it, right?"

She fiddled with the hem of the wool jacket, quiet for so long, I didn't think she would answer.

When I pulled in front of my flat, she finally lifted her head and met my gaze, her eyes serious. "I understand you're not being rude, but you don't know me at all, so I'm not dear to you. I'm not your love."

I put the car in park and killed the engine. Rain beat down on the roof, sounding louder in the silence between us. I really didn't know what to say to that except to respond truthfully. "I would like very much to get to know you better."

Her eyes softened, and for the first time, I noticed the flecks of gold hiding in the brown. I framed her face with my hands and pulled her in for a kiss. She didn't resist, but I kept it light and easy. But then she whimpered, gripped my shirt, and dragged me closer.

I angled her head and coaxed her tongue to dance with mine for a brief moment, then lifted my head. "Want to make out in the car like teenagers?"

Those big brown eyes twinkled playfully. "Absolutely."

Her lips sought mine, and her arms snaked around my neck.

The rain raged on, but the only thing I heard was the beating of my heart and our combined heavy breathing. I fumbled for the button on the side of my seat, and the backrest began to recline. I dragged her with me until she lay across me and the console separating us.

"Wait." She climbed over it and straddled me, and we both sighed as her pussy centered on my dick. Her hair veiled our faces, concealing us from the world.

She wiggled her hips and reared back. "Oh, that's different."

I cocked a brow. "It's the same as it's always been."

A grin parted her lips. "I mean the silk lining of these pants against my…" She laughed. "Oh my God, I have to tell you, someone ripped off my panties last night."

"You don't say." I grinned.

"I do say." She arched, undulating her hips. "And during my meeting it hit me that I was sitting there with strangers, and I didn't have on any underwear."

My dick pulsed, and my hips jerked. "Jesus, lu—Dani—you don't know how much my tongue envies your pants right now. I am going to eat that pussy as soon as they come off."

She shuddered. From my promise or the cold? "Well, they're not coming off out here."

Taking in the fogged windows, I doubted anyone could see inside even if they were stupid enough to be out in this weather, but the cramped space wouldn't allow for what I wanted to do to her. "Let's get you inside."

I sat up, and her head hit the ceiling. She laughed as she crawled off my lap and back to the passenger seat with me dodging her elbows and knees. "This isn't as easy as it was in high school."

I'd had my share of backseat sex, but I didn't want to hear about hers. I reached for the umbrella in the back seat. "I'll go unlock the door then come back for you."

"What's the fun in that? I'm already wet." She jumped out of the car and ran around the back end.

I jumped out and ran to catch up with her, umbrella open, which was pretty useless in the downpour. She laughed again and huddled against me as I unlocked the front door.

Once inside, I dropped the umbrella into the stand. "Stay here. I'll get some towels."

"No!" She grabbed my arm as I started for the stairs. "Oh my God, don't track water on these floors." She began to strip.

"I like the way you think." Peeling my T-shirt over my head, I watched her remove the pants and jacket. As she said, she'd gone commando. The wet, white blouse clung to her tits, the sheer fabric clearly outlining the black bra encasing them.

A hard jolt of need slammed into me, vaporizing all concern for her well-being. I backed her against the wall and dropped to my knees.

She laughed. "I knew you had a thing for options, but walls? Must be an architect thing."

"I have a *thing* about *you* against walls."

Gripping her hips, I wedged her in place and lowered my mouth to the soft skin above her mound. I glanced up to find her watching me and jutted my chin at the soaked blouse. "Take it off."

Whipping it over her head, she shed the bra as well. Her eyes narrowed with lusty anticipation, then suddenly grew wide. "Wait, I'm wet."

"I hope so, or I'm doing something wrong." Teasing her bellybutton with my tongue, I inhaled deeply, and the scent of her feminine arousal swirled in my head.

Threading her fingers into my hair, she tried to push me lower. "It'll ruin the wallpaper."

"Fuck the wallpaper...and the floors." I kissed my way to the small strip of hair, spanned my hands wide, and used my thumbs to open her slick folds. She was drenched, and not just from the rain. Her little button, hard and swollen, glistened in the gray light. "I need to taste you."

Danielle

AN EXPLOSION OF HEAT burst through me as Michael's tongue glided through my folds and flattened against my clit. Melting against the wall, I moaned and tightened my hold on his hair. "Do it again."

He grunted and lifted one of my legs over his shoulder. "I plan to."

Lapping and licking, nipping and sucking, he coaxed me close to the edge of orgasm.

"Twist your nipple," he commanded, his finger rimming my entrance.

One hand still firmly clasping his hair, I pinched the taut bud at the same moment his finger plunged deep. He began a slow pistoning in-and-out action. The friction was delicious, causing my pulse to quicken. He pulled out, then doubled up on the next drive in, stretching me, filling me, curling against my G-spot, and...over I went with a keening cry, into the abyss of mindless bliss.

He continued thrusting and sucking, prolonging my pleasure until I floated like a feather on a soft breeze, back to reality.

I looked down at him as he took one last swipe with his tongue, gifting me with a sweet jolt of aftershock. He withdrew his fingers and sucked them into his mouth one at a time. My pussy clenched. How could I possibly crave more?

How could I not? I finally had the man of my dreams—and a million fantasies—touching me, tasting me, wanting me. It was fucking surreal.

"That was even better than I'd hoped," he said, licking his lips.

"Definitely." I eased my leg off his shoulder and let go of his hair. "Sorry if I pulled too hard."

"I loved it." He stood, dug his wallet from his back pocket, and pulled out a condom.

"Nope." I grabbed it from him. "Let me."

Smiling, he toed off his shoes and shucked his jeans and underwear before I was on my knees. I sat back on my heels and looked at him. "God, you're beautiful."

All sinewy with grooves cut to define every muscle. Hair sprinkled between his pecs, and a dark feathery trail sent my focus to the thick shaft roped with pulsing veins. A trickle of pre-cum wept from the slit of the broad head.

Curling my fingers around the base of his cock, I rose on my knees to lick the tip but stopped short and peered up at him.

Stormy gray eyes watched me intently from beneath heavy lids. "You don't have to ask for my permission. I'm in."

A bubble of laughter died before it escaped as I bent to flick my tongue over the spongy tip. His salty essence rolled over my taste buds. Another glance up at him, all dark and enthralled, encouraged me to lick around the ridge, lubing the hot, velvety skin before taking him into my mouth.

A long breath escaped his lips, and he rolled his hips to slide deeper. He gathered my hair from my face with one hand and used it to pull me closer. "Feels so good."

His praise spurred me on, and I concentrated on transforming that *good* to fucking spectacular. Angling my head, I took him to the back of my throat until my lips met my hand. Swirling my tongue along the length, I swallowed.

His hips pumped forward, forcing me to open my throat, but he quickly backed off, and I took up a slow in and out, bobbing my head and twisting to give him as much tongue action as possible. Pausing on the in, I held him as deep as I could, for as long as I could. On the out, I sucked in my cheeks.

"Bloody hell." He moaned. "Take it all. Suck harder."

His fingers fisted in my hair, pushing and pulling. He thrust faster, his breathing harsh. I kept up with his tempo, holding onto his thighs for balance. His excitement incited mine. Making him want more made me want to work harder to please him.

And I wanted to ride the high with him. I reached between my legs.

"No." Using my hair to hold me in place, he backed out of my mouth. "I want to come inside you. Put the condom on me."

I grabbed the condom, opened the wrapper, and encased his cock in one easy roll. Before I could blink, he hauled me up from the floor and walked me backward a few short feet into the living room. He stopped behind the sofa, spun me to face it, and placed a hand between my shoulders, guiding me over the back.

"Spread your legs." His cock teased my entrance, and his fingers dug into my hips. "I hope you're ready. I can't wait."

Hands braced on the cushioned seat, I tilted my hips, wiggled against him, and peered over my shoulder. "Then don't."

Plunging hard and deep, the tip of his cock hit just the right spot. I moaned. "Fuck."

He didn't give me time to adjust, but I didn't need it. My pussy was dripping wet and hungry for the man I'd wanted for too many years. I didn't need or want gentle.

As if reading my mind, he slammed into me, harder, faster. His balls slapped against my clit, heightening the pleasure.

"So...fucking...good." Each word was punctuated with a hard thrust. "Don't...want...it to...end."

Neither did I, but the tightening in my core warned me I was close. I reached between my legs to strum my clit but lost my balance. I slapped my palm back on the cushion to keep from falling.

He hissed and gripped me tighter. "I've got you. Do it. Make yourself come."

Trying again, I found my center and rubbed. Heat blossomed from my core and spread like wildfire through my body. My inner walls clutched at him, making the friction of his thrusts even more delicious.

"Harder," I begged.

He pounded into me, and when I shuddered through the last of the earth-shattering orgasm and lay my head on the cool leather, he grunted, lodged deep, and roared his release.

I'd never felt so thoroughly fucked. Or aware of my partner. Michael surpassed all my fantasies and then some. But at what cost? I knew myself well enough to know I wouldn't walk away from this weekend unscathed.

This scenario of Michael not knowing my true identity had been better than any plan I'd come up with to seduce him. I could have my fantasy and make a quick exit without him ever knowing my feelings for him went beyond a silly girlhood crush.

Last night and tonight and maybe tomorrow night, I'd give myself over to him. Eventually, he would be ready to move on to someone new. And I would go back to real life and become a forgotten notch on his bedpost.

Chapter Six

Michael

I HUMMED AS I CLEANED the mess we'd made last night. Danielle's purse had fallen on the floor, the mirror over the table hung at a crooked angle, and one of my wellies lay beneath the table. I righted the mirror, placed her purse on the table, and stood the boot by the umbrella stand with its mate.

After gathering our clothes from the floor, along with her lacy wisp of a bra and the little black number she'd used to sop up the rain, I moved on to pick up the blouse and wool suit she'd worn to her meeting. She was right. The suit was ruined. But it would be worth every penny to replace it. And I would replace it because *she* was worth it.

I glanced at the living room, and my dick swelled at the memory of bending her over the sofa and pounding into her hot, tight little pussy. She'd enjoyed the rough sex as much as I had.

Afterward, though, I'd carried her upstairs

and wrapped myself around her soft body to sleep for a couple of hours before making love to her—slow, sweet, and easy as if we'd done it a million times. She'd woken me at dawn, straddling my hips, taking me deep, and riding me into heaven.

We'd passed out again, sleeping until midmorning when I slipped on a pair of shorts and a T-shirt, crept from the room, and headed downstairs. I could easily imagine spending my days and nights like this. I'd never felt that way about a woman, only with Danielle.

The doorbell rang as I laid our damp clothes on top of the dryer. I hurried to the door so that whoever it was wouldn't push the bell again and wake her.

When I opened the door, I was surprised to see my mother. I opened the door wider. "Mum, get out of the rain."

She ducked inside. "I won't stay, but the rain slowed some, and I thought Danielle might need something to wear besides her dress and the suit…in case she hasn't found her keys."

"You're the best." I kissed her cheek as I took the bag from her and set it on the entry table. "She's still asleep, but if you can wait, I'll wake her. I'm sure she'd love to thank you properly."

"No, no. I'm having an early lunch with Deborah."

"Well, hold on. Let me get the umbrella, and I'll walk you out."

"Wait." She placed a hand on my arm. "Michael, I don't want to be an interfering mother, but there's something different about you, a sparkle in your eyes that hasn't been there since before your father and I went our separate ways. I've always blamed myself for stealing that light from you."

"No, Mum, don't ever blame yourself." With an arm around her shoulders, I pulled her in close and kissed the top of her head as guilt lodged in my chest. "We've talked about this. You tried with Brandon, but it was a battle best walked away from. And you are not to blame for my hang ups."

"That's just it, darling." She pulled back to look up at me. "I have never considered your search for love a hang up." She stepped away and smoothed her blouse. "What I'm trying to say is that you seem happy and...content for the first time in a very long time."

I looked at the stairway as if the topic of our conversation might appear, then returned my focus to my mother. I couldn't stop the grin that stretched from ear to ear. "I think I've found her."

She smiled through watery eyes. "That's wonderful."

"Mum, don't cry." I could never stand to see a woman cry, especially my mother. She'd done too much of it in my youth.

"Happy tears, darling. Happy tears." She brushed them away and looked at her watch.

"Well, then. I'll leave you to it and be on my way."

"I love you, Mum."

Shit. Fresh tears welled. "I love you, too. Now, let me get out of here before my behavior puts this downpour to shame."

Chuckling, I opened the door, then stopped to put on my wellies. Something stabbed my big toe. I pulled my foot out and reached inside. Whatever was in there was stuck. It finally came loose, and I withdrew...a set of keys with a keyring stating the owner was Britain's bitch.

"Are those the infamous missing keys?" my mother asked, her hands clapping silently.

My chest tightened, and my heart stalled. "I guess so."

They certainly weren't mine, but I recognized the key ring. And if I was right...

I looked up the stairs again.

"Oh, lovely. Now, everything is set to rights."

"Yeah," I murmured, nausea swirling in my gut.

"Well, I should go."

Somehow, I managed to walk my mum to her car without throwing up, but as she drove away, shock and confusion glued my feet to the sidewalk.

There were millions of key rings like the one I'd found. It didn't have to be Dom's, the one I'd given him to celebrate the closing of his new home, the one that said Dom was *Britain's Bitch* now that he'd signed his life away on a mortgage.

Unable to shake my suspicions, I stood there another long moment, rain soaking me to the bone, before I turned slowly toward the house, dragging the umbrella behind me.

Absently, I slogged into the house and closed the door. I didn't want to believe it. That Danielle could be Dominic's sister Daisy.

My gaze fell on her purse, and I swallowed. If I called the number Dom had texted to me...and her cell rang...I couldn't go back. I couldn't unknow the truth. That she'd been lying to me.

My heart pounded harder, faster. Was it all just a game to her? Was she playing me? I didn't want to think so. She seemed to genuinely like me and want to be with me.

Fuck. Bile rose in my throat. If I called Daisy's number and it turned out to be a coincidence...

"Bloody hell." I dug my phone from my jeans and found Dom's text.

The number glared back at me in black and white, possible evidence that the whole time she'd been with me she'd been lying. I tapped the line of numbers, held my breath, and stared at her purse, willing it to be silent. Through the line, I heard Daisy's phone ring.

A millisecond later, Danielle's purse vibrated, and my heart sank. After four rings, voicemail picked up. "This is Danielle Russo.

Leave a message at the tone."

My fingers tightened around my phone, and I wanted to throw the damn thing across the room, but that wouldn't do anything to appease the hurt firing my anger. Why'd she do it? What did she have to gain by lying? The attraction still would have been undeniable. Dom's sister or not, I'd still have wanted her. Wouldn't I?

I'd always gone with my instincts, and they'd never let me down. While Danielle had her secrets, my gut told me there wasn't a mean bone in her body. Her emotions were real, her heart sincere. And I hadn't missed the way her eyes softened when she looked at me. She'd cried during sex, for fuck's sake. Didn't that say something?

The fucking silence in the room wasn't reassuring, but the way I figured it. I had three options.

I could give her the fucking keys, call her a fucking cab, hustle her ass out of my life and never fucking see her again. That idea scared the shit out of me. I'd waited a long time to find her. I didn't want to let her go.

Some of my anger dissipated as I dismissed option number one.

Option number two was to give her the keys and ask her to stay so that I had time to convince her we had something special. If she realized that, hopefully, she would confess her deceit and tell me why she'd lied. That was a good option.

The last option was a bit riskier. I could lay the keys by her purse, wait for her to find them, and see what happened. She'd either say *"It's been fun."* Or she'd want to stay without me having to ask. I wanted the decision to be hers.

Risky for certain, but I'd already made it plain in telling her I wanted to get to know her. It was time for her to decide what she wanted. That didn't mean I wouldn't do everything in my power to fucking lead her toward my way of thinking.

Blowing out a long breath, I laid the keys beside her purse and went back to the laundry. The ball was in her court.

Danielle

ONCE AGAIN, I FOUND myself wearing Michael's white dress shirt and on my way down the stairs to find him. I smiled at how we couldn't seem to make it inside the front door before devouring each other.

Something smelled delicious, but I was hungrier for him than whatever he was cooking. But before I got too busy getting busy in the kitchen, I needed to check for any news from the museum or Dominic. Funny, I hadn't given either much thought once the interview was over. Michael had stolen my every thought. And my heart.

Who was I kidding? It had always been his.

As I drew closer to the table in the entryway, my tummy took a tumble. A set of keys lay beside my purse. Dominic's keys. My gaze snapped toward the kitchen, but a short wall blocked my view of the stove. I could hear him humming.

I glanced back at the keys and swallowed hard. He'd found them and obviously put them here for me to see. So that I'd leave? My excuse to stay no longer existed.

But I wasn't ready to go.

Nerves jittering, I dropped the keys in my purse, grabbed my phone, and scrolled through the missed calls. Making time to call Dominic was a priority. The most recent call was a number I didn't recognize. A London number. The museum?

I flipped to my messages. One of them, another London number, had to be from the museum.

Unknown: *The job is yours. Call Monday at your convenience.*

This was the reason I'd come to England in the first place. I should be overjoyed, dancing in my underwear...if I had any to dance in. But taking the job meant living in the same city as Michael, possibly running into him and seeing him with someone else on his arm.

I didn't want to think about that right now, though.

Stuffing my phone back into my purse, I looked into the mirror and blinked, barely recognizing the woman looking back at me. My skin glowed, my hair was a wild untamed mess, and my eyes shone like a woman well and truly fucked. No, it wasn't just a random fuck. I was happy. Happier than I'd been since…ever.

All the alarm bells clanged in my head, screaming at me to run before my heart shattered into pieces. But it was too late to save my heart. Either, he'd break it, or he wouldn't, and I'd have to live with the fallout. Until then, I hoped Michael would share a little more of himself with me.

With a sigh, I walked into the kitchen. He looked up and smiled, and my tummy did a flip that knocked over a whole breadbasket of butterflies. And the way his gaze traveled over my legs…

"Good morning," I said tentatively as I drew closer, trying to gauge his mood other than the obvious arousal narrowing his eyes on my tits. I'd left all the buttons on the shirt undone except one.

Just because he wants to fuck me doesn't mean he wants me to stay.

Shut up.

"More like afternoon." He handed me a cup of coffee. "Are you hungry?"

I arched a brow over the rim of the mug. "Very."

He turned back to the stove to mash the toasted bread oozing cheese. "Food first, or we'll die of malnutrition in my bed."

"I was thinking about the kitchen counter." I patted the marble covering the large island.

He groaned and hauled me against his hard frame with one arm. His mouth brushed mine lightly. "You are definitely asking for it."

"Would you prefer me on my knees, begging?" I ran a hand over his chest, loving the play of taut muscles under the faded blue T-shirt. "Because that can be arranged."

"Oh, I'd love you on your knees, but your beautiful mouth would be too full to do any begging." His tongue lapped at my lips, and a zing rippled from my nipples to my clit. He tasted of coffee and mint and Michael. His hand slid under the shirt and palmed one cheek, then slapped my ass.

"Yow!" The playful swat startled me but didn't really hurt. Heat bloomed across the injured cheek and melted into my core.

With a quick kiss, he set me aside. "You're going to make me burn lunch."

The lingering sting had me rubbing my ass as I wandered to perch on a stool. "Mmm, spank me, Daddy."

He barked a laugh and pointed his spatula

at me. "Behave or I just might."

"Promises, promises."

"Cheeky wench."

Giddy with the hopefulness of the playful banter, I watched him expertly flip the grilled cheese in the skillet. My stomach growled. I couldn't remember the last time we'd eaten. We'd nibbled on apples and grapes at one point, but that seemed ages ago.

Michael seemed happy to have me hanging around his kitchen, albeit half naked. And he was cooking for me. That was a good sign.

"Where did you find the keys?" I ventured.

"In my wellie."

"Ouch, that sounds painful," I quipped and squeezed my legs together.

He rolled his eyes but grinned. "Wellie, not willie."

I knew perfectly well what he'd meant. I simply loved making him smile.

I shrugged. "If you say so."

The kitchen settled into a comfortable silence for a few minutes, him plating the sandwiches, me watching him and trying to memorize everything about him, every mannerism, the long fingers that played so well over my skin, the cock of his hip, the tilt of his head. Everything. Like I could ever forget.

Gearing up my courage again, I asked, "Are you free this afternoon?"

His gaze met mine over his mug. Something flickered in those stormy depths. Relief? Maybe.

But his whole body seemed to relax. He shook his head, his eyes twinkling with mischief. "No, afraid not. I'll be spending it with a woman who has a sassy mouth and killer legs."

"And what will the two of you be doing?"

"Well, for starters, I'll be *doing her*...on this island." His nod encompassed the white slab of sleek marble as he ladled tomato soup into a small bowl as if he were talking about gardening.

Heat rushed to my core and slickened the inside of my thighs as I imagined myself lying on the cold stone, Michael between my legs, pumping that delicious dick into me. I almost squirmed in my seat. "Oh? tell."

"Actually," he said, his tone turning serious, "if you don't have anywhere to be, I would like to take you to my favorite place in London."

Leaning an elbow on the counter in disappointment, I rested my chin in my palm. "Unless it's in this house, I can't go." I waved a free hand to indicate his dress shirt barely covering my body. "No clothes."

"Mum brought a change of clothes for you this morning."

I sat up straight. "She did?"

Nodding, he placed a plate of grilled cheese and a bowl of tomato soup in front of me. "Or, since we now have your keys, we can go by your place to get some of your clothes."

I shoved the sandwich in my mouth and took a big bite, trying to figure a way out of his suggestion. Take him to Dominic's? No way. When the answer came to me, I swallowed a lump of cheese. "Are you kidding? Who wouldn't want to wear something your mom designed?"

The light in his eyes dimmed a little as if he were disappointed in my answer. I couldn't imagine why. Unless he wanted to know where to dump me later. No, no, no. I wouldn't let my insecurities ruin the time I had left with him.

Still, I couldn't help feeling I'd somehow let him down.

Shoving aside my doubts, I slid my leg against his under the counter. "So, you think I have killer legs?"

Danielle

"IS THIS APPROPRIATE for your favorite place?" I twirled at the foot of the stairs for Michael's approval. I'd used his brush, braided my hair, and tied it off with a rubber band I found around the celery in the refrigerator. Nothing I could do about makeup, so I scrubbed my face clean.

His gaze slowly roamed my body before settling on my face. "You're perfect."

The jeans Laura had chosen fit like a dream. The blouse, a soft pink with tiny white flowers, had long flowy sleeves that poofed and gathered at the wrist. The sheer gauzy material revealed an underlying white cami. I'd ditched the black bra, but the cami was tight and held the girls in place.

The only thing that didn't fit with the ensemble was the stiletto sandals. First thing, wherever we went, I was buying a pair of flats.

Michael handed my purse to me, and I looped it over my head, so the strap rested diagonally between my boobs and the clutch settled on my hip. He grabbed my hand and wove his fingers with mine, his excitement infectious as he swept me out the door.

Instead of heading to his car, he walked me up the sidewalk. I matched his long stride to keep up with him and grimaced at the pinch of my sandals. "Are we going to your mother's again? Is that why we're walking?"

He gave me a funny look, then my meaning seemed to catch up with him. "Right. Mum's house isn't far, and I did tell you I like to walk there, but no. It's a bit farther where we're going."

"Not that I'd mind spending time with your mom," I explained. "She's a fascinating woman. I just don't think these shoes were made for hiking. I need to stop somewhere to buy something comfier."

"Not to worry, lu—sorry." He slowed his

pace. "Where we're going has everything you could ever need."

"You're being awfully mysterious."

"We all have secrets, but you'll know mine as soon as we get there."

I chewed my lip as I sank deeper into the pit of deceit I'd dug myself into. I wanted to tell him everything and hoped he'd understand, but I just couldn't risk losing the precious and quickly diminishing time I had with him.

A couple of blocks from his house, he stopped at the corner. "I'm going to leave our transportation up to you. Would you rather take the underground or ride the bus?"

"Hmm, the underground sounds intriguing, but I don't want to be down in the dark. I want to do the touristy thing. I want to see the city."

"Double-decker it is, then." He pointed to one of the iconic red double-decker buses pulling up.

A few minutes later, we were seated on the upper level. Michael had given me the outside window so I could take in the view.

"Will we be able to see Big Ben? Or London Bridge? Or the Thames?" I asked without taking my eyes off the passing cityscape. "And the Tower? Can we see that?"

He leaned close, his chest to my back, one arm along the back of my seat. "Only if we go in the other direction. We'll see those another day."

Another day? My insides churned and my heart ached.

I felt an overwhelming urge to kiss him quiet, to beg him to take me back to his house, to lock the world away so there was no need for words that couldn't be said with our bodies. Because whether I stayed in London or not, my time with Michael was running out.

Michael

"THERE." I POINTED as the bus bumped along Kensington High Street, Danielle's enthusiasm rubbing off on me. It was like seeing the city I adored through new eyes again—her eyes. I wanted her to love it as much as I did. I couldn't wait to show her all of London and its countryside. Wherever she wanted to go, I'd take her.

If she got the job and moved here from the States.

I didn't want to think about how I'd feel if she didn't. "That's Leighton House. You might find it of interest if you're into art history." I kissed the back of her slender neck. "You like art, right? I mean, we met at the art exhibit."

She shivered and tugged the sexy braid out of the way, inviting me to taste more of her, yet

I wasn't unaware of how her shoulders stiffened at the subtle opening for her to finally trust me and tell me the truth. "Yes, I-I do love art."

I sat back in my seat, ignoring the tightening in my chest. Perhaps she didn't trust me. Dom had a hard time trusting anyone that first year at uni. We'd been assigned as dorm mates and were well into our second semester before Dom let his guard down. It had taken another year before he opened up about his family situation.

It stood to reason Danielle might have the same issues with trust. I just needed to be patient.

The double-decker jumped on the A3220 North and skipped along, and in a matter of minutes, we were approaching the Westway Roundabout where traffic picked up.

I glanced at Danielle and smiled at her nose practically mashed to the glass like a kid looking in a candy store. "Our stop is coming up."

The bus finally pulled over at the corner of Cambridge Gardens and Portobello Road.

"This is us." I slid out of the seat and into the aisle, backing up so that she could go ahead of me.

When we stood on the sidewalk, she looped her arm through mine. "Out of all the places in London, this is your favorite?"

"It is." I covered her hand with mine and led her up Portobello Road to the first clothing shop.

"Let's see if they have any shoes."

Fifteen minutes later, a pair of flat, white sandals lay on the counter, along with a large Union Jack bag.

"To carry my heels in," she said, "and anything else we find."

I pulled out my wallet, but she handed the cashier a card.

Her gaze slid to mine, and she shook her head. "Thank you, but I pay my own way. You and your mom have done enough."

She was definitely as proud as Dom. Too many times, he'd missed out rather than accept anyone's "charity."

As we wandered down the row of multi-colored tents and buildings, stopping at each vendor, I wasn't sure we'd make it to the end before dark. We'd gotten a late start, and Danielle oohed and aahed and touched everything. She chatted with people from all walks of life peddling their wares. We explored everything from books and jewelry to vintage clothing and antiques. It was a good thing her new bag was big because she'd stuffed it full of homemade soaps, candles, and shampoo.

"Gifts for back home," she offered.

Finally, an opening I'd been waiting for. "Family?"

"No, just friends and co-workers," she said, her tone taking on a cautious edge as she turned away to thumb through a book. I wondered if she even read the title or saw the words on the pages before laying it back down.

"So, you know a lot about me—where I live, what I do. You've even met my mum." I picked up the same book, flipped it over, and pretended to read the blurb. "Are you going to tell me anything about yourself?"

She picked up another book. "I thought we agreed that a woman is allowed her mysteries."

"I never really agreed, and you did say I was welcome to uncover as many secrets as I could."

Hugging the book to her chest, she turned to look at me from beneath thick, black lashes, in a shy but seductive way that made me forget what we were talking about. "I'd say you've uncovered quite a lot." She lowered her voice. "By now, you know almost as much about my body as I do."

As she'd obviously intended, my cock stretched to fill out my jeans. As much as I'd like to resolve that problem behind one of the tents, I wouldn't be deterred by sex, which seemed to be her go to for keeping me distracted. "What's your last name? Can you at least tell me that?"

"I can tell you my middle name is Anne."

I blew out a breath of frustration. "That will do...for now."

Laying aside the book she'd been clutching, she turned away and exited the tent. The sun had crept low on the horizon, casting shadows from the buildings onto the road. Streetlights flickered on.

I followed her to the next awning, but she

didn't linger over the colorful scarves. Her eyes had lost their sparkle, and her teeth gnawed at her lower lip. Bloody hell, I'd wanted her to enjoy our outing, and now, I'd upset her.

Grasping her elbow, I pulled her to one side of the sidewalk and tugged her in for a brief kiss. "I'm sorry. I only want to know more about you."

A sadness in her dark eyes cut me to the quick before she blinked it away and attempted a smile "I know."

She didn't offer more, so I let it go and tucked her arm in mine. "Let's get something to eat."

I knew who she was. That would have to be enough until she was ready to trust me.

Danielle

"WAKE UP. WE'RE HERE." Michael's deep voice roused me from a dream.

Lifting my head from his shoulder, I tried to get my bearings. It was dark, and we were in the back of the rideshare he'd called. We'd both been tired and full from a delicious Italian meal, but the mood between us had changed. We hadn't recaptured the ease we shared all weekend.

As we'd crawled in the car after dinner, I only meant to close my eyes for a few minutes, but with his arms around me, I'd snuggled closer, savoring the feel and scent of him. But the weekend had caught up with me, exhaustion stealing what could be my last moments with him. And now, I wasn't sure where we stood or if he would want me to leave.

I'd ruined everything. I could have made up a last name. I almost had. But I was determined not to lie to him any more than I already had.

The driver pulled to a stop in front of Michael's house, and I slid out of the car behind him. Once inside the front door, we took off our shoes, and I padded barefoot behind him into the kitchen where he placed our to-go boxes in the fridge.

I pulled fruit and cheese from the bag, along with some of the homemade hand cream. "Will you see that your mother gets this? It's not much, but she was so kind and generous."

When he didn't answer, I looked up. He was doing that quiet thing again that unnerved me. Standing at the sink, his arms braced on the white porcelain, he stared out the window into his little backyard.

Perhaps I really had overstayed my welcome. The bridge of my nose burned at the thought of leaving tonight. It would be hard enough to leave in the morning.

Hoping I was wrong, I rounded the island and slipped my arms around his waist. I laid my cheek against his back and listened to his heart beat. "Do you want me to go?"

He stirred from his musings and turned to face me. Leaning against the sink, he spread his legs and pulled me between them. One hand palmed the side of my neck, his thumb grazing a path of desire along my jaw. The butterflies in my belly fluttered their tiny wings, but a cold veil of anxiety weighed them down.

Solemn gray eyes tracked his actions for a moment, but now, they searched mine. "Do you want to go?"

"No." I bit my lip to keep it from trembling and held my breath.

"Then stay." He lowered his head, and his mouth feathered over mine.

The kiss was tender, sweet, and agonizing all at once. This would be my last night with Michael.

I tightened my arms around him and pressed my body against his, suddenly desperate to show him how I felt since I couldn't tell him. He palmed my ass and dragged me against his hard erection.

Easing back, I murmured against his lips, "Make love to me, Michael."

He groaned and swept me into his arms. He carried me through the kitchen and living room and up the stairs, eating at my lips the entire way. Stopping at the foot of the bed, he slowly lowered my feet to the floor and tugged my shirt and camisole over my head. I shoved his T-shirt out of the way, so I could kiss his chest as I started on the button and zipper of his jeans. With one hand, he reached behind his head and yanked his shirt the rest of the way off.

Thought took a backseat to instinct as I drew the denim down narrow hips and long, muscular legs. His cock sprang forward, and I reached for the velvety shaft.

His fingers manacled my wrist. "Not this time."

Before I could blink, Michael lifted and tossed me on the bed. "Jeans off."

With trembling fingers, I unbuttoned my jeans, but he yanked them off before I got them unzipped. Crawling backward up the bed, I had time to catch a single breath, and then he was over me, nudging my knees apart, the head of his cock nudging my entrance. His mouth slanted over mine as, inch by inch, he drove forward, stretching my inner walls in slow abandon, filling me...completing me.

I lifted my legs so that my knees rode against his ribs. He slid deeper.

He tore his mouth from mine in a strangled growl. "Bloody hell, you feel so fucking good."

"Mmm."

"I forgot a condom." It sounded more like a question.

"I got the shot." My core clenched around his hard-as-steel cock.

His face contorted. "I've never gone without a rubber, but if—"

"Same." With a tilt of my hips, I encouraged him to move. I needed the closeness to him just this once...one final time.

Resting on his elbows, he started a leisurely rhythm. His lips parted mine in a hungry kiss, his tongue taking up the same deliberate pace, and I drowned in the turmoil of overwhelming emotion—joy, despair, love.

Then the delicious friction sparked, and I lost myself to the building fury. Hotter and hotter, like a storm of fire in a chasm just out of reach, the all-consuming pleasure lured me to its edge.

His hand found my breast, squeezing once before his fingers pinched and rolled the taut bud. I dove headfirst into the unforgiving flames of pure bliss. Every nerve ending sizzled and lava poured through my veins.

Somewhere beyond the vortex of fire, Michael's guttural roar echoed in my ears. Pulsing hot jets of cum filled me, creating sweet jolts of aftershocks. If I turned to ash, it wouldn't matter, as long as he was with me.

Too soon, awareness snuck around the corners of my subconscious, dousing the glowing embers. The sound of our heavy breathing, the smell of sex, the wetness between my thighs. And the calming weight of his muscles settling on top of me. I drank it all in until reality invaded and I remembered I'd never feel this way again.

I felt the familiar sting behind my eyes as he eased to one side and took me with him, so that we lay together in a tangle of limbs, skin to skin, spent, a fine sheen of moisture coating our bodies. Silent tears slipped from my tightly clenched eyes as I waited for his breathing to slow and his body to grow lax.

When I was sure Michael slept soundly, I eased from beneath his possessive grasp. Hovering over him, I brushed a lock of tawny hair from his forehead and bent to kiss his cheek. "I love you."

His lips curled upward in a wicked smile. For a moment, I thought he'd wake, but his mouth relaxed and his breathing evened.

I slipped out of bed, leaving the jeans and blouse where they lay on the floor, and tiptoed downstairs to find the dress I'd worn to the gallery Thursday night. God, it seemed so long ago, and yet it had gone by so fast...too fast.

Heart pounding, I found the dress on the washing machine and tugged it over my head. As it fell into place, I hesitated only a second before grabbing Michael's white dress shirt from the top of the pile. I held it to my nose and breathed him in. My heart panged, screaming at me to go back upstairs, to crawl into bed, and steal as much time as I could with him.

Instead, I let my feet carry me to the kitchen where I shoved the shirt into the Union Jack bag and crept to the front door. I slipped into my flats, and with a hasty glance at the stairs, I asked myself for the thousandth time if leaving this way was the right thing to do. Once again, the answer was no, but what else could I do?

Tell him the truth.

Michael would never understand my reasons for keeping secrets, for lying. This was the best way for both of us. He could move on, no doubt with a sigh of relief. And I wouldn't have to feel the crushing blow of rejection, of being unloved, of...

Turning away, I opened the door and stepped into the purplish light of dawn.

Chapter Seven

Danielle

I WAITED UNTIL I WAS at the corner before I called a rideshare. Dozens of notifications of calls and texts from my brother rolled up the screen, but I couldn't deal with them right now.

Ten minutes later, I was on my way to Dominic's, separating myself from Michael one row of blurring townhouses at a time. The tears I'd been holding back broke loose and fell unheeded down my cheeks.

God, why does it hurt so much?

"Are you all right, luv?" the driver asked. "Can I help with anything?"

I shook my head. No one could. I'd made a mistake, one I would both regret and cherish for the rest of my life. Sure, I could go back and tell Michael the truth. He wouldn't be mad. I didn't mean enough to him for that kind of reaction. We'd gone into the weekend with no expectations. It was only supposed to be a quick fling. A fantasy.

To me, though, it had been so much more.

He'd always been more, but he was so much more than I'd imagined. Hot AF and great in bed, but he was also smart and funny. And charming and sweet and kind and thoughtful.

And you're temporary, one of many.

Hiccupping around another sob, I clutched my bag tighter. It was over. Time to cut my losses and move on before I was in too deep.

Too late.

I'd fallen hard, and there was nothing I could do. Right now, all I wanted was to be alone, to curl up on Dominic's sofa with Michael's shirt and cry until it was time to catch my flight. Where I belonged. There'd be no dream job. It wouldn't mean anything without the dream man.

The car stopped in front of Dominic's house, and the driver handed me a tissue. "I hope it gets better, luv."

I choked out a thanks as I climbed out. I wanted to be Michael's *luv*.

As I tried to fit the key in the lock, the door swung open, and Dominic filled the frame. "Where the hell have— What's wrong?"

I brushed past him, not up to his questions. "Nothing. I'm fine."

"You're fine? You don't look fine." He shut the door with a soft click that belied the concern rolling off him in waves and piled on the guilt. "And I'm sure as fuck not fine. I've been worried out of my fucking mind. Where have you been all weekend?"

I shrugged and shook my head, unable to speak around a fresh round of tears lodged in my throat. I turned away, knowing I looked a mess. There was no denying what I'd been doing.

"Daisy, talk to me." Dominic caught up to me and turned me to face him. "And don't lie. The fridge is still full, and"–he pointed to the stairs—"you haven't slept in your bed. Then you come home distraught. What's going on?"

"Calm down."

"Don't tell me to calm down."

My last thread of energy surging to life, I wrenched free of his grasp. "I'm a grown-ass woman. I'm not accountable to you. You're not my fa—"

I clamped my mouth shut, and shame washed over me like yesterday's dirty dish water. Dominic had been brother, mother, and father to me for most of our lives. He didn't deserve my anger when it was really directed at myself.

Another flood of tears spilled onto my cheeks. "I'm sorry."

"Come here." With an arm around my shoulder, he led me to the couch and sat beside me. "I'm sorry, too. I'm lashing out at you when I've got my own shitstorm brewing."

"What's wrong? Are you okay?"

He shook his head. "You first."

I looked down at my lap. He'd always been the one I turned to, but now I wasn't sure I should. "I...met someone."

"Here? In London?"

I nodded.

"You hooked up with a stranger?" He sat back, concern marring the sharp angles of his face. "I can't believe you'd do that. I mean, you know I'm not judging, but... What if he'd been a serial killer, Daize?"

He might as well have been. *I feel like I'm dying.*

I turned to stare out the window without actually seeing beyond the memory of Michael's gorgeous smile and smoky-gray eyes. "He was perfectly normal. And sweet and thoughtful, and the sex was amaz—"

Dominic slapped his hands over his ears. "Lalalalalalalalala, I do *not* want to hear about you having sex."

I attempted a faint smile, wiped my face, and blew my nose into the soggy tissue the driver had given me.

"Then why are you crying?" He folded his arms across his chest. "What did the bastard do?"

"He didn't do anything. I did. I screwed up. I lied to him."

"What did you lie about?"

"Everything." Another fucking sob stuck in my throat.

"Okay, start at the beginning."

I sighed. "I ended up going to the art exhibit after all."

I went on to explain how I met someone at the art exhibit, about losing his keys, how he helped me get to my interview, and that I'd fallen head over ass in love. I omitted a few details, like what I lied about, the intimacy we'd shared, and Michael's name. Telling Dominic who he was would only jeopardize their friendship, and I couldn't live with that.

By the time I'd finished the story, I was blubbering again.

Gathering me in his arms, Dominic held me tight, rocking me, soothing me with nonsensical assurances that it would all be okay. It wouldn't. I wouldn't. Not for a while, anyway.

When I'd exhausted myself into silence, he drew his head back to look at me. "If it makes you feel any better, I screwed up, too. Sarah and I had a fight, and I left."

"You left her there alone with her father at death's door?" I pushed at his chest and his arms fell away. "It must have been one hell of a fight."

"It was." Now, it was his turn to stare out the window, and all I could think was that he might have been emotionally absent for Sarah because he'd been so preoccupied with worry when I didn't answer my phone.

"What did you fight about?" *Please don't say me.*

He flopped back on the sofa and rubbed his eyes with the heel of his hands. "Fuck, I don't even remember."

"You don't remember what the fight was about, or you don't want to face the real reason you fought?"

"It was..." He got up to pace. "It was stupid and"—he smacked his chest hard—"and all about me and my insecurities."

I nodded. This I could understand. Abandonment and neglect had done a number on both of us.

"It just seemed that as soon as we got to South Africa, she didn't need me anymore. I tried to be supportive, but I..." His tanned cheeks flared red, and he stopped pacing to look at his feet. "I felt useless and in the way."

"I'm sure you weren't. If I know anything about you, it's that you always put others above yourself."

"I was so used to having her all to myself. I was...jealous." He waved aside the words about to spill from my mouth. "I know, it's ridiculous, and I'm ashamed to say it. I talked her into going down to the cafeteria to eat, and on the elevator ride down, I made the mistake of suggesting we go to her parents' house to get some rest. But in my defense, she was dead on her feet. She hadn't left the hospital in two days."

"You were thinking of her."

"I was, but...I don't know. Maybe because I was holding her in the elevator when I suggested it and she felt my... Fuck, I can't help it if I get hard every time I touch her."

Hands over my ears, I sang, "Lalalalalalala."

Dominic laughed, and his mood seemed lighter. "Anyway, she accused me of trying to get her alone for sex, which I wasn't, and that led to an argument. She told me to leave, so I did. Then all I could think about on the flight home was whether she actually made it to the cafeteria to eat."

"Yep, you're a real ass."

"I know."

"I'm kidding." I shook my head. "Dominic, it was probably her fear and uncertainty about her father's condition that caused her to lash out."

He sighed. "Yeah, I realized that after I calmed down."

"So why are you still here?"

Planting his hands on his hips, he lifted an accusing brow. "I booked a return flight as soon as we landed, but I came home to check on you first and found you gone."

For just a moment, I'd lost myself in Dominic's pain, but now, my own problems came rushing back. "I'm so sorry."

He sank down beside me again and took my hand in his. "Daisy, if this guy you met is so great, why can't you just explain whatever it is that you lied about, say you're sorry, and live happily ever after?"

"Because I know him—er, his type. He's a player. He used me to get rid of his flavor of *last* week." Just saying those words sliced at my heart. They had been so easy to fling at Liz, and now, I'd become the cliché.

"Are you sure? You said the time you spent with him was good. Sounds like he was into you. Sometimes, things aren't always as they seem."

I tugged my hand from his. "You're supposed to be on my side."

"I am on your side, but if what you shared was so special, you owe it to yourself to think about all the possibilities."

"Like what?"

"Okay, for instance, maybe he's not really a player. Maybe he's just afraid of getting his heart broken."

"Like you?"

"Yes, like me. In the heat of the moment, I let the doubts I'd had when I met Sarah creep in. I felt like Sarah was only with me because she didn't know anyone here in London. I was just a fill-in until she could get home again to her friends and family."

"Dominic." I gave him my best *shame on you* face.

"I know." He held up his hands. "Let me give you another example. You remember Michael, right? I mentioned him the other day."

I stiffened but managed another nod as my heart began to beat faster.

"He's as confident as a person can be without being conceited, and anyone who doesn't really know him would think he's a player...like your guy."

Nausea rolled in my belly. *He's not my guy. Will never be my guy.*

"His dad tries on women like clothing and discards them just as easily. He's been married and divorced more times than you can count on one hand. Because of that, Michael won't let himself commit to a relationship for the sake of not being alone."

"I don't understand how that isn't the same as being a player."

"He believes it's not fair to let a woman become invested if he's not going to do the same. Claims one date, sometimes less, is all it takes to know if she's the one or not, and he'll go on searching until he finds his Miss Right. And when he does find her, he'll move heaven and earth to keep her."

Fuck. I thought I was all cried out, but fresh tears pricked my eyes as I processed Michael's perspective. How was it any different from women dating men until they found the right match? Why would I be free to do so, but not Michael? I'd been such a fool.

Talk about a double standard.

"Granted," Dominic went on, "Michael's a good-looking guy. He's confident, and women flock to that shit, so it makes him look like a player. But he's not." He chuckled. "Honestly, I thought he was delusional, but that's exactly how it was for me when I met Sarah. I don't want anyone but her."

The events of my weekend with Michael

replayed in my mind. His consideration. How he'd been so patient when I was lashing out because I couldn't find Dominic's keys. How he'd involved his mother and made my interview possible. And yesterday, at the market, women couldn't keep their eyes off him, yet he never seemed to notice.

From the very beginning, he could have called a locksmith and a cab and said, *"See ya."* But he hadn't.

Instead, he wanted to get to know me. He wanted more time with me, more than one night.

That didn't mean I was Michael's Miss Right. But Domonic made a good point. I owed it to myself and to Michael to try. "I've made a big mistake."

He nodded. "We're a pair, aren't we?"

I jumped off the couch. "I've got to go."

"You might want to change first. You're looking a little...worn."

"Good idea." A warm feeling of home lifted the corners of my mouth...and my heart. I hadn't realized just how much I missed Dominic and our heart-to-hearts since he left New York. "I'm so glad I'm going to have you around more."

Surprise widened his eyes. "You got the job?"

"I got the job."

He scooped me up in a hug. "That's so great."

Dominic's ringtone filtered down the stairs. He dumped me on the sofa, and I laughed as he took them two at a time to answer. Shaking my head, I went upstairs to shower and change into something that didn't smell ripe.

I'd have just enough time to swing by Michael's place before my flight. Hopefully, I could convince him to forgive me and give me another chance before I said goodbye for a couple of weeks.

I only hoped Dominic was right about Michael. Either way, when I flew home today, I'd be leaving my heart in London.

Michael

WARMTH SLICED ACROSS my face as light snuck through the cracks in the blinds. I reached for Danielle, but the sheets beside me were cold. Levering up on one elbow, I looked at the clock. Seven a.m. I scanned the room. Her clothes were on the floor beside mine.

I flopped back down on the bed. She'd probably stolen my T-shirt. She seemed to like wearing my shirts. I certainly liked seeing her in them…and taking them off her.

Swinging my legs over the edge of the bed, I sat up and stretched. I rose, did my business in the bathroom, and brushed my teeth to avoid offending her with a morning kiss. More than a kiss if I had anything to do with it.

I slid into a pair of shorts, gathered up our clothes, and headed downstairs.

"It's your turn to cook breakfast," I called out as I rounded the newel post.

I stopped at the opening to the kitchen. The emptiness of the space reached out to punch me in the gut. The bag she'd left on the island was gone. I turned around to check the entryway. The shoes she'd purchased yesterday were gone. "Goddammit."

I dropped the clothes and ran up the stairs to make sure I hadn't missed her. A search of the empty rooms told me what I feared most but what I already knew. She was gone, too.

Just like that. No note. No goodbye. Nothing. But why? Why wouldn't she give me at least that? She'd given me fucking little else besides the best sex of my life.

Wrong. In the brief time I had with her, she'd awakened a part of me I feared I'd never find, much less feel—love.

Oh, I loved my mum and begrudgingly my father. I loved Robert as a surrogate father. And Dom as a friend. And a few other relatives I couldn't remember. But loving another person with my whole heart, mind, body, and soul...

Yeah, and then she'd fucking walked away as if our time together meant nothing. She obviously didn't feel the same way I did.

You can't make her love you.

No, I couldn't. And I'd done all I could to convince her to stay...and to tell me the truth. And still, she'd left.

My mind went blank as reality truly sank in. I sat heavily on the edge of the bed, and the scent of her perfume and our lovemaking drifted from the sheets to envelop me. But rather than soothe me, it pissed me off.

I stood and ripped the sheets from the bed, only to sink onto the mattress and bury my face in them, trying to suffocate the hurt and anger raging inside me.

I couldn't think, couldn't breathe. Numbness would be preferable to this indescribable and foreign ache in my chest. It was like treading water during a storm and being dragged under.

"Fuck." Tossing the sheets back on the bed, I stood and crossed to the dresser for a T-shirt. I shoved my feet into my sneakers. I couldn't be in the house. I needed to move...do something. A run would help drive her from my mind.

Like that's possible.

Better than fucking sitting around, wallowing in self-pity and this feeling of desolation.

You could go after her.

If she'd wanted me to go after her, she'd have told me who she was, where to find her, and that she wanted to explore this thing between us, whether she got the bloody job and moved to England or not. But no, she'd run off like a child.

As I passed the table in the entryway, I saw the jar of lotion she'd wanted my mother to have. I stuffed it in my pocket and hesitated, my hand on the doorknob. I looked back at the house that I thought I'd made a home. I'd been wrong.

In the short few days Danielle had been in my life, *she* had been the one to make it feel like a home.

And now, I wanted to take a sledgehammer to my fucking favorite wall.

Chapter Eight

Michael

"OH, SWEETHEART, I'm so sorry."

I sat at my mother's kitchen table after pouring out my story to her. Not everything. Just the basics. My run had burned off the anger, leaving a huge ache in my chest, and I desperately needed her advice.

"Though I have to admit," my mother said, darting a glance between me and Robert, who stood against the counter eating a breakfast sandwich, "I didn't know either until after you two left here. She'd said something odd, and I couldn't stop thinking about it."

I spun the jar of cream on the table. "What did she say?"

"She was looking at your picture gallery on the stairs. She said she was 'just going down memory lane.' After you left, I went to look at the photos and saw the one of you and Dom. That's when it hit me. I could see the resemblance between Danielle and Dom. He kept me company a lot when I came to visit you.

He showed me pictures of her. Of course, she was only a girl back then, but..." She shrugged. "Anyway, I'm sorry I didn't say anything. I thought you knew."

I grunted and gave the jar another spin. "Guess that's what I was to her. Just a trip down memory lane."

"No, darling." She took the jar from my hands and placed it to one side. "I don't think it was that at all. Her feelings were written all over her face when she looked at you. That girl adores you."

I sat back against the chair. "Then why wouldn't she tell me?"

"You lived with Dom for four years," she said. "You already know the answer to that question."

I did. Or I'd thought I did. "It's just... She seemed so brave, so bold, so...confident."

"I think she is all those things. But she's also a woman who's had her fair share of disappointment and heartache growing up." She referred to the things I'd shared with her about Dom. "I'm not excusing her for leaving without saying goodbye, but to me, it sounds like she was afraid of rejection or you being angry with her."

"I am angry." *And hurt.*

My mother crossed her arms. "Actually, I'm not sure what difference it makes whether she told you or not. You knew who she was after you found the keys, and you didn't say anything to

127

her about it. You lied by omission."

"But I didn't know until after I found the keys. She knew who I was all along," I grumbled, knowing my logic was skewed and not quite fair.

Robert looked up and pinned me with a fatherly gaze that said he was about to impart something profound or philosophical, and I wasn't going to like it.

"Only two things I want to know, son." He swiped crumbs off his hands over the sink. "First one is, do you love her?"

"Yes." But was it really that simple?

"Okay, that answer makes the second question relevant." Robert crossed the kitchen to stand behind my mother. He placed his hands on her shoulders. "If you've been waiting for her all this time and if you love her, what the hell are you doing here? Why aren't you going after her, fighting for her?"

I shot out of my chair. "If she'd wanted me to come after her, she would have told me how to find her."

"Robbie's right." She patted Robert's hand. "You and I both know it was difficult for me to trust after your father. I didn't ever want to let myself love a man that way again. That meant getting hurt. But Robbie didn't give up on me, and I've never been happier. Perhaps Danielle needs a little pursuing."

My stomach twisted as my mother's words hit home. I remembered how hard it was to watch Robert pine for her when she shut him down and to see the fear and hesitance in her, especially when they obviously loved each other.

Was that all it would take to win Danielle? Was it up to me to be strong, to be the one to risk everything for what we could have? If she truly didn't love me, yes, I'd be lost, but at least I would know I'd done everything in my power to win her heart.

I looked at my watch. "She might already be on her way back to the States."

"You've said many times you'd move heaven and earth for the woman you loved." Robert waved a hand. "Catch the next flight out. Go after her."

"Yes." My mother beamed with excitement. "You can get her address from Dom. It won't be as if you're looking for a needle in a haystack."

I looked at Robert. "Will you take care of my schedule?"

"For as long as it takes."

"Thank you both." I kissed my mother and hugged Robert.

"Keep us updated?" my mother asked.

"I will."

I sprinted home to pack, book a flight, and call a rideshare. As I was about to shut the door, I took another look at my home. Moving heaven and earth to keep the woman I loved was a tall order, but if I had to leave London and move back to the States, I'd bloody well make it happen.

Darah Lace

Danielle

PASSPORT IN HAND, I waited in Dominic's kitchen for the taxi I'd called to take me back to Michael's. I traced the UK stamp with my index finger. I'd have to work on getting my work visa if I accepted the job offer at the museum. I was still undecided.

Disappointing Dominic would be hard, but knowing I could run into Michael at any given moment scared the hell out of me, especially if things didn't go well when I confessed the truth.

"Wish me luck." Dominic picked up his backpack.

I looked up at him. "You won't need it. Just be honest and open with her."

"Like you're going to be with your guy?" He adjusted the pack on his shoulder. "Are you ever going to tell me who he is?"

"Depends on how it goes when I tell him...stuff."

"Text me and let me know." He gave me a mock frown. "And I mean it. Don't leave me hanging."

I nodded and gave him a hug, then he

hurried to the front door. I checked my phone to see if my ride was close. Nope, but that gave me time for a snack to settle my stomach. My nerves were shot.

The front door squeaked open as I peered inside the fridge.

"Hey, man. I'm on my way out, but Daisy's here."

Who was Dominic talking to?

The low, rumbling response answered my question. *Michael.*

I slammed the fridge shut and met his gaze over Dominic's shoulder. My throat went dry. God, he looked good. And he didn't seem at all surprised to see me here.

"She's on her way out, too, but she got the job, so she'll be back," Dominic rattled on, not realizing I heard every word. "Well, maybe. She hooked up with some guy this weekend and fell in lo—"

"Dominic!" I wanted to crawl in a deep, dark hole and never come out. Oh, wait. I'd already dug that hole, and I was supposed to be climbing out of it.

A soft smile lifted the corners of Michael's sexy mouth. "Is that right?"

Dominic turned to look at me, then at Michael and back to me. His eyes narrowed. "He's the guy?"

I pinned Dominic with a hard gaze, hoping to convey my need for him to let me handle my own shit. "Please, just go."

"All right, all right." He turned back to Michael. "If you break her heart, I'll kick your ass."

Michael's gaze never wavering from my face, he nodded. "Duly noted." As the door shut behind Dominic, Michael added, "So you got the job."

My heart pounded against my ribs. "I did."

"Are you going to take it?" Was there a hint of hope in his eyes?

"That depends."

"On?"

I wavered. Telling him would make it final. He'd either accept my apology or reject it...me.

"You...me...us. Whether you'll let me explain. I can't live here knowing our—" I swallowed around the desert in my mouth. "That what happened between us might affect your friendship with Dominic."

"It won't."

"Maybe not on your end, but Dominic..." A thought struck me hard. What was he doing here when Dominic was supposed to be in South Africa? "It's not a coincidence you're here, is it? That you just showed up here?"

"It isn't," he snapped. "I came to see you, though you certainly didn't make it easy."

"You're mad." *Of course he's mad. You knew he would be.*

"Damn right, I am." He stalked toward me. "You left without a word, as if what we shared, as if *I* meant nothing to you."

Despite the urge to back up, I stood my ground. "That's not how it was."

"How was it, then? Because that's certainly how it felt."

"I— Wait. You knew who I was?"

Some of the accusation in his stormy gray eyes disappeared, and a flush stained his cheeks. "Yes."

"How long?"

"Long enough."

I placed my hands on my hips. "Michael, how long did you know?"

He sighed. "Since the morning I found the keys."

All the conversations after that moment, all the questions, his moodiness... "You were trying to get me to tell you?"

His lips thinned, and he quirked a brow. "Ya think?"

"I thought you were—" I bit my lip to keep it from quivering.

His expression softened, and he moved closer, almost but not quite touching me. He lifted my chin with a forefinger. "You thought I was what?"

"When you went off into your thoughts and got all quiet..." I closed my eyes, unwilling to let him see how much it hurt to say the words. "I thought you were ready to get rid of me."

"Why would you think that?" He thumbed my cheek to wipe away a stray tear.

I opened my eyes. "Because I thought you

were a player."

"I wasn't the one playing games or keeping secrets. Well, not in the beginning. But even after I knew who you were, it wasn't a game. I thought if you really wanted to be with me, you'd tell me the truth."

"I couldn't, not in the beginning because I..." I lowered my gaze to stare at the logo on his T-shirt. "I used to have this big crush on you when you and Dominic were roommates. When you flirted with me at the exhibit, I thought I could finally act on all my, er, fantasies about you."

He chuckled. "You had fantasies about me?"

My gaze flew to his, and relief poured through me. He wasn't mad. I let myself smile for the first time since he arrived. "Yes, lots of them."

"Hmm, we'll have to examine those fantasies, but later." He settled his hands on my hips. "You were saying?"

"Right." Unsure what to do with my hands, I rested them on his biceps. "The first morning, I realized what I'd done, the mess I'd made. I was going to sneak out, but then I couldn't find Dominic's keys, and—"

"Thank God for that."

"—then you were so sweet. You went out of your way to help me, and you seemed to want me to stay. I couldn't possibly tell you the truth. I wanted to be with you for as long as I could. Telling you was a risk I wasn't prepared to take. I thought you'd be angry or that being Dominic's sister might muddy the waters, and you'd send me away."

"You had it all figured out then."

"No, not at all." I tried to push him away, but he wouldn't be budged, so I dropped my forehead to his chest. "I'm so sorry. It's all a mess. Believe me, falling in love with you was not in the plans."

There. I'd said it. Now, it was up to him.

My phone pinged, but I ignored it, waiting for Michael to say something, anything.

Another ping.

"You should get that."

So that was it. Without saying a word, he'd said it all. I pulled the phone from my back pocket and checked the screen. "I have to go. My taxi is here."

"Weren't you going to my place?"

"Yes, but I really should get to Heathrow. My flight leaves soon."

"I'll be right behind you."

I jerked my head up. "What?"

"I'm not letting you out of my sight again." He sighed. "I know you'll think this sounds ridiculous, and you probably won't believe me with all your trust issues, but I've been waiting a long time for you. The fact that we just met makes no difference. I love you. I want us to figure out what we have together."

"You do?" I'd hoped he'd give me a chance to win his heart, but... "Really?"

"I do. I can't breathe without you, luv. I'm

going to New York until you sort out whatever needs sorting, so you can come back here with me." He placed a finger on my lips to stay the words bubbling to the surface. "And when I call you luv, I want you to know I mean it."

"I was only going to say that maybe I could move my flight so we can go together."

Ping.

"Dani, you need to get rid of that taxi, so I can kiss you properly."

I quickly fired off a text to let the company know I didn't need a ride and to charge me for the time the driver had been waiting plus a healthy tip. Curling my arms around his neck, I whispered, "Now, where were we?"

Instead of kissing me, he said, "Ask me again what kind of girlfriend I want you to be."

I frowned. "That was not where we were."

"Ask me."

"Back to options, are we?" I muttered and heaved an exaggerated sigh. "Okay, what kind of girlfriend do you want me to be?"

He grinned. "Well, if my options are still the same, I could choose between the serious, clingy, totally in love girlfriend or the one who's only in London to get lucky. Right?"

"Right."

"Well, I changed my mind. I want the serious, clingy, totally in love girlfriend, but only if she's you."

I melted against him, my palm sliding along his oh-so-hard dick. "What if I still want to get lucky in London?"

"I don't think you have anything to worry about." Michael brushed his lips over mine. "My question is, will I be getting lucky in New York."

~*~

Thank you for reading
Getting Lucky in London.
For up to date news of my coming soons,
free goodies, excerpts from my current work
in progress, and other announcements,
sign up for my newsletter at:
https://www.darahlace.com/newsletter/

Darah Lace

About Darah Lace

I live in Texas where I enjoy a simple life with my husband and two dogs. I love sports—it's really all about men in tight uniforms—music, anything artistic—painting, cake decorating, home renos, makeovers, etc.—watching a good romance, and penning scenes that sizzle. When I'm not writing or reading, you can find me at one of two places—my day job (blech) or a bookstore looking for my next adventure.

Connect with Darah

darah@darahlace.com
https://www.darahlace.com/
https://linktr.ee/darahlace
https://www.amazon.com/author/darahlace
https://www.goodreads.com/darah_lace
https://www.bookbub.com/authors/darah-lace
https://www.tiktok.com/@darah_lace_author
https://www.instagram.com/darahlace/
https://www.facebook.com/darahlace/
https://www.facebook.com/DarahLaceAuthor
https://x.com/DarahLace

Sign Up for Darah's Newsletter
https://www.darahlace.com/newsletter/

Also Available
Bachelor Unmasked
Preston Brothers Book One
By Darah Lace

He wears a disguise to discover the truth.
She wears one to keep secrets.

After a long business trip, the last thing Spencer Preston wants is to attend a masquerade party. His plan? Get in and get out. However, an encounter with a hot she-devil changes his mind, especially when the woman behind the mask is the no-nonsense secretary he's been fighting an attraction to for months. Suspicious of her dual lifestyle, he dons a mask and sets out to discover her secrets.

Melody Jamison hates hiding behind her plain-Jane persona, but her last job ended in sexual harassment. To get a promotion at Preston Enterprises, she needs to show Spencer she's more than a pretty face. The problem is, she's hot for her boss. When a friend suggests a masquerade is the perfect place to be herself without revealing her secrets, she agrees to a night out. She never dreams she'll meet a masked stranger who makes her body hum like only Spencer can.

There's a corporate spy running loose at Preston Enterprises, Melody is at the top of the suspect list, and Spencer must continue to hide behind a mask in order to uncover the truth.

Other Books by Darah Lace

COWBOY ROUGH SERIES
Saddle Broke
Bucking Hard
End of His Rope
Taming the Wildcat
Texas Two-Step
Deal with the Devil (Coming Summer 2026)

PRESTON BROTHERS SERIES
Bachelor Unmasked
Bachelor Auction
Bachelor Bad Boy (Coming Summer 2025)
Bachelor Betrayed (Coming Fall 2026)

MACTYRE VALLEY WOLVES SERIES
Claiming Sophia
Embracing Everly (Coming Winter 2025-26)

STAND ALONES
S.A.M.
Falling into Darkness
Yes, Master